FLARE OF VILLAINY

THE IMDALIND SERIES, BOOK 10

REBECCA ETHINGTON

Published by Market Street Books LLC

Copyediting by C&D Editing
Production Management by Market Street Books

ISBN (print) 978-1-949725-50-6
ISBN (e-book) 978-1-949725-42-1
Printed in USA
This Edition, June 2021

❋ Created with Vellum

THE COMPLETE IMDALIND SERIES

BOOK ONE: *Kiss of Fire*
BOOK TWO: *Eyes of Ember*
BOOK THREE: *Scorched Treachery*
BOOK FOUR: *Soul of Flame*
BOOK FIVE: *Burnt Devotion*
BOOK SIX: *Brand of Betrayal*
BOOK SEVEN: *Dawn of Ash*
BOOK EIGHT: *Crown of Cinders*
BOOK NINE: *Spark of Vengeance*
BOOK TEN: *Flare of Villainy*

THE ACADEMY BOOKS
The Gauntlet
Rogue Royalty
Broken Renegade
Reluctant Seer

Find me online in my Facebook street team! We have monthly giveaways, sneak peeks, competitions and more!

1

RYLAND

"No surprises this time, okay?" I pulled Jos close, whispering the words in what I hoped sounded like a warning. She just grinned at me and pulled back, turning toward the crowd that had gathered in the great hall of Imdalind for the council.

"No promises."

She was still smiling, but neither that or the reason we had called the council here was going to do anything to calm my nerves. I felt as though I was going to explode. I needed to get out of here. I needed to save Míra. We were wasting precious time with these meetings and as much as Jos promised me she was going to be okay, I didn't believe it. The council needed to approve this, and we needed to leave.

I already felt coiled tight enough to explode.

Before Jos could even get a word out, however, a gasp and a sob echoed from the back corner of the council hall, from the exact place Wyn had said the Americans were. The panic in the sound was only pushing me closer to the edge.

Jos turned, clearly wondering what was going on, but I didn't have an answer any more than she did. Another cry pulled her focus, and we all stepped to the edge of the dais, Wyn and Thom's faces as panicked as mine.

"Everything okay over there?" Joclyn called, her voice wavering as the shocked cries turned to whispers of panic.

"No, I'm sorry my Queen," someone responded, their voice breaking. Bodies shifted as everyone made way for the American that was rushing towards us, phone already extended.

Damn it. Something had clearly happened.

When Joclyn jumped off the stage to meet the approaching man, I was only one step behind, magic rushing right to my fingers in case this ended up being some stupid attempt at an assassination.

But no, it was a sobbing man with a cellphone. Not that that was any better. He flashed the phone at her, the message and its following news article blazing in brilliant color.

'Kyō take White House! Extermination order given!'

I had only just finished reading the headline when every phone in the vicinity began to go off. One after another they buzzed and sang, people pulling them out of their pockets to look in horror at the screens.

"Fuck!" I should have known, with the way that bastard talked. So much for killing him. It didn't do a damn bit of good.

"The Kyō have taken the United States," Joclyn said, her voice loud even though I could hear it shake. "We must move quick--"

"It's not just the United States!" someone called from the back, and everyone turned as an older Chosen with greying red hair held out his phone. Even from here I could see it. "They took Brazil!"

"Mine says Russia!"

"Spain!"

"South Africa!"

"England."

Countries echoed around the room as one after another phones were lifted, news articles displayed as the worldwide takeover by the Kyō became clear.

Suji wasn't kidding when he talked about his divine right to rule. He had clearly already granted himself that right.

"How is this possible?" Joclyn hissed, looking from phone to phone as she spun in the quickly deteriorating crowd. Their mood had shifted from shock to panic, the emotions growing more volatile as they began to read the articles and exchange notes on what was happening in their countries. The crowd was quickly turning into a powder keg.

I looked from Jos to Wyn, who glared at me with the same ambivalent shock that I felt. After what we had seen in the house on Trafalgar Square neither of us were surprised by this. I should have bet on those bastards trying to take over the world. I would have made a little bit of money. You know, if money still had any value.

"You need to take control of this," I whispered to Jos, my voice low in her ear as I led her back to the dais. "We need a plan."

"How are we supposed to devise a plan against an army who likes to suck the power out of the Chosen?" Jos hissed, hands waving through the air as we jumped onto the platform, forming a tight little circle in the middle of the madhouse.

"Easy. We calm them the fuck down and devise a plan against an army who uses the Chosen's magic as their sole energy source," I said, glaring at my best friend. She knew she was letting that Queenly facade slip. Now was not the time.

"You two killed the leader, you saw what they were doing, how do we end this?" Thom asked, looking between Wyn and me as the crowd began to yell for the doors to be opened and the war to begin.

Screw a powder keg, they were going to be an atom bomb if we didn't do something fast.

God, if Ilyan was here he would have already fixed this. Probably just flown into the Kyō's headquarters and kicked all their asses on his own or something.

"First, we clearly didn't kill the leader of the Kyō or this wouldn't be happening," Wyn began, holding up her finger on the half with a hole in it so that it looked like an exclamation mark. "Second, I am a million percent sure that those governments did not *fall* to the Kyō. They probably handed over the keys nicely."

"She's right," I said, glancing at the crowd and angling myself between them and Joclyn a bit better. "Suji said that he was working with the United Kingdom, that they were already in control. But those articles say that it was just taken over today. They offered them electricity, the governments took it and--"

Joclyn held up a finger, cutting me off as she twisted to the crowd that was little more than a mob now. They screamed at us, raging as they pumped their fists in the air. It was probably good that the magic of the council stopped them from attacking.

"Thom," she whirled back around, Thom jumping at the mention of his name. "Do a search, find out which countries they *didn't* take control of." Thom nodded and turned away, already tapping on his phone. "Wyn, I'm going to need you to release the shield on the hall the second I am done. We are going to need everyone to get out of here."

"What? And attack you?" Wyn folded her arms. "Ry and I are good, but we aren't that good."

"So dramatic. Don't worry, I've got this." Jos winked at her before turning back to the raging faces and panicked expressions. I tried to keep myself at an angle in front of her, but she wasn't having it.

Okay, shield it was. She sure made playing her bodyguard difficult sometimes.

"Quiet!" Joclyn yelled in Czech, the magic in the word silencing everyone instantaneously and leaving them only able to throw daggers with their eyes. Which they did.

"As you all know, the Kyō have taken control of most of the countries on our globe, and have called for the capture and destruction of the Chosen. I have Thomas checking on locations that might not be affected." And the 'Queen' voice was back. Jos was firm and confident. Too bad it only made everyone else even more ragey.

"For now, I need you to know that the Kyō is who Ryland and Wynifred fought while on a mission for me in the United Kingdom. We have seen what they are doing to the Chosen, and why these extermination orders have been given." The more she talked, the more they calmed, and the more I was reminded of just how much of a powerhouse she was. "The Kyō will not be executing the Chosen. They will be rounding them up and using them as weapons to keep their crown." She paused, everyone looking horrified as they glanced at me and Wyn.

"We've seen it!" Wyn yelled, and for once she actually sounded sick. "They are sucking the magic out of them. It's how they have their power. We need to protect the Chosen if we want to defeat the Kyō."

"I know many of you are wishing to go after the Kyō right now," Joclyn continued, "and we will. But first we must take away the power at its source. We must save the Chosen!"

Thank God everyone roared in agreement as she finished. With how her speech started I wasn't sure we would get much more than eye daggers; but they all stomped their feet and clapped their hands excitedly.

I didn't feel any of that emotion. I only felt dread.

I needed to save Míra; but, I knew Jos was right, even if I felt all angry about it. Even Wyn, who flanked Joclyn on her other side, was looking energized.

"Go to your home countries, bring *all* of your people here. This may be the last safe haven, and we need to use it until we have made our world safe again. Once we are gathered, then we will plan, and as one we will go after the Kyō! We will take back our world and make it safe for everyone, magic and non-magic users alike!"

More clapping, more stomping, and more cheers of approval. Jos gave Wyn a nod and in a wave the shield fell from the hall, the doors swung open, and everyone ripped out, bowing to Joclyn as they fled.

Hopefully, they would retrieve their people and return. With how everyone was scowling and stomping however, I had a bad feeling it was much worse than that.

"Is it just me, or did you just declare war on the world?" I asked, the knot that had been in my stomach since Míra's disappearance growing.

I knew we wouldn't be going after the SSU from the second the first report was shouted across the hall. But, to hear the plans change, knowing that it was taking us further away from her broke me for some reason. I was sure it broke Jos, too. It wasn't just Míra we had been planning to rescue. They had been so close, but with one news story they were gone.

That fun loving girl of the last few minutes had been instantly replaced with the stoic battle Queen that she had built by shoving all of that hurt and pain down.

I didn't think I could let her do that.

I didn't know how she did.

2

RYLAND

Latvia. Ukraine. Georgia. China. And, of course, Japan.

Those were the only countries that had not been in the news about some takeover by the Kyō. Australia had been in the news last week about a hostile takeover, images of battles plastered on news outlets for days. But everything else was peaceful, or in the case of those five, nonexistent.

The Kyō started in Japan and very quickly spread to China, so those two being excluded from the reports made sense. From everything we could piece together, the Kyō had already been there for the last year or so. But Latvia, Ukraine, and Georgia did not fit that bill.

Which meant only one thing.

"That's where the SSU are," Jos said, tiptoeing her fingers over the map. "They don't already have control of those countries. If I had to guess, and seeing as we know the SSU to be there, they are going to go down much the same way Australia did."

"In a blazing ball of fire!" Leave it to Wyn to be excited about that.

I didn't miss that Jos's trek over the surface of the map ended with her pointer finger right against Kiev, Ukraine. Right at the hospital we were so certain Ilyan was.

Where Mira could be.

The spot seemed haunted with the way the shadow of her hand flickered over it. The lamps that surrounded the map turned all the lines into wobbly monsters, of course that might just be me seeing things thanks to the fact that we were all up way too late after helping talk down many of the regional leaders from just going after the Kyō themselves.

If we were going to stop them from doing that we needed to have a plan in place before they returned. I was really starting to regret not having slept at all when I was in London the last few days.

"So, the Kyō are going to attack the SSU. Wouldn't it make more sense for us to attack the SSU, then force them to submit and be prepared for the Kyō when they arrive?" Thom asked, his brow furrowed as he looked over the map, all of us focusing on the spot in Kiev. He wanted our brother back as much as I did.

"Yeah, it's what Ilyan would do." Wyn nodded to Thom. "Battle planning must be in your genes."

"Either that or I've sat in on enough of these meetings over the years," Thom deflected and I chuckled.

I knew the types of meetings Thom was talking about, although I am sure when Thom sat in on them they were more heavy battle planning rather than planning the espionage missions that I was always sent out on. Either way, they were all focused around our father's need to kill Ilyan.

Thankfully, he had failed at that in the end.

"So have I, but I just wanted to go in and kill the leader." Wyn shrugged, pointing to the town in Japan that the Kyō were supposedly centered around.

"That's what everyone else wants too." Jos finally removed

her finger from over Kiev and instead ran it over her ribbon. She wasn't looking at anyone, just at that spot on the map.

The same heavy weight that had lived around her right after Ilyan had gone missing had returned, sucking away the light that had returned to her eyes only hours before.

Just seeing her fall back into that pit was making my heart ache. I stepped closer.

"So? If going after the SSU is the right choice, then we do that. They will all come along," I said. Her shoulders didn't even lift.

Her eyes were dark as she looked at us, jaw set, everything in her wound like a coil.

"They won't though," she hissed, still rubbing her finger over the ribbon as she looked at me. "They want to take out the Kyō once and for all, and to them that means cutting it off at the head."

"Makes sense," Wyn mumbled, shrugging.

"But this way we get Ilyan back," I said, tapping the map over Kiev a bit too firmly and sending the lights flickering again. "Surely they can see that?"

"They would if they knew him." Jos's dark eyes bored right into me. "You know that all these regions are made up of the Chosen, often led by only one or two Skřitek, and sometimes none at all. They don't *know* Ilyan. To them, he is a legend, a guy from a picture that's five years old--"

"And one we can save!" I snapped, interrupting her as I poked at the map again.

That time, she jumped. I knew I should feel some kind of regret for my outburst, but I couldn't. Not with the way I was literally watching her soul break in two, again. Not with the way my own heart was cracking.

I wouldn't let her go through this. Not when we could stop it.

"You think I like this, Ryland?" she snapped, slamming her palm on the table and sending one of the lanterns tumbling. Wyn barely caught it, mumbling something about letting her deal with all the fire while Jos and I stared each other down.

"We can save him, Jos. We know where he is. Let the Chosen go after the head. We can find Ilyan, and then we can end this. Together." I was firm, confident. I tried to grab her hand, needing her to know that she was not alone, that we would fix this. Instead, she pulled away.

"No."

"No?" I jerked away from her so quickly I sent the lanterns rattling again.

"These are my people, Ry. *Our* people. I cannot just abandon them to go find... to go save..." She pressed her lips together, glaring daggers at me in an attempt to hide her pain.

I reached out again and this time, thankfully, she let me grab her. I wrapped my arms around her the way I always had, holding her against me as she breathed, as her magic pressed against mine. The fiery touch of it, the caustic iciness that had lived between us for so long now just a friendly simmer.

"You can't keep sacrificing yourself like this," I whispered into her hair.

"What if we do both?" We turned. Wyn stood there, raising her hand like she was in elementary school, both she and Thom looking smug as though they had planned this all along.

"What if we get Ilyan before we head to Japan?" Wyn continued when neither Jos nor I said anything. "Say you two head to Kiev, take out the SSU before the Kyō get there. Rescue Ilyan... and Míra," she added when my brow furrowed. "Come back, and then we all go to Japan and finish this off. End all the regimes, and take over the world."

Wyn grew louder as she continued to lay out the plan before laughing like one of the villains you saw in old movies. I probably would have been scared if I didn't know Wyn so well. Somehow 'evil woman villain' suited her.

"Why am I not surprised that you want to take over the world?" Thom teased as he threw his arm around Wyn, pulling her into him.

My stomach flip-flopped, of course evil Wyn would turn Thom on; it's how he knew her.

"I've always fancied myself as Queen Empress Supreme," Wyn teased, kissing Thom on the nose before turning to where Jos and I stood on the other side of the table. Jos was grinning like a loon, I was starting to feel like I was going to vomit.

"I mean, of course, I'll have to fight Jos for it but--"

"Oh no!" Jos cut her off, hands in the air. "I resigned my title and gave it to Ryland, remember?"

"Leave me out of this!" I roared, throwing my hands up, too. Jos and I looked as though we were being held at gunpoint for the crown. Maybe we were.

"Don't worry, we all know it's Ilyan's crown and I don't have a big enough head to try to take him on." Wyn grinned, Thom giving her a look that clearly said she *did* have enough air in her head to think she could take Ilyan on.

"So, what do you say?" Wyn continued, still ignoring Thom. "Shall we go get them?"

All of the weight that had been on my heart fell away, even Joclyn straightened.

"Once everyone has arrived here," Jos began, her fingers trailing over the map again as she pointed right at Prague, or rather the caves of Imdalind that were right outside it. "Wyn and Thom can train, organize and supervise while Ryland and I go here." She moved her fingers to Kiev and I could have sworn my heart attempted to explode right out of my chest. "We will get Ilyan, find Míra, and do whatever we can to the SSU. After that, we all go to Japan and end the Kyō. Then Wyn and Ilyan can fight for the crown of world emperor."

"Empress," Wyn corrected her.

I smiled, I couldn't help it. We were going to go save her. *Them*. We were going to go save them.

"I hate to bring up anything against this great plan," Thom said, pulling down Wyn's victory stance, "but do you think you two can take on everything on your own?"

I half expected Joclyn to sag beside me, but she just smiled wider, leaning over the map to stare him down.

"I found my mate, Thom, do you really think I would let anything as simple as a massive Trpaslík army stand between me and Ilyan?"

Thom wasn't even phased by her death stare. He just smiled and leaned over the table towards her, both of them so close as they scowled at each other that I had to fight my bodyguard instinct to pull Jos back.

Not that she couldn't take him on anyway, not with the fire that was in her eyes.

Not with the fire that was rippling from her magic.

"You're right, nothing is going to stop you."

3

MÍRA

IF I HAD PICKED a way to spend my seventeenth birthday it would not have been tied to a hospital bed in the middle of Ukraine.

I wasn't a hundred percent sure it was my birthday, but it had to be close. It had only been about a month away when I followed Ryland to London, and seeing as I woke up in a grungy hospital room and not the nasty train I had been knocked unconscious in, more than a few days had to have passed.

So, birthday it was.

I blinked away the throbbing headache that I was starting to think was a symptom of whatever meds they were pumping me with and tried to sit up. No go.

I was strapped down like I was in a mental asylum. Great.

It's where you belong.

Had to hand it to him, I couldn't really argue with Edmund that time seeing as he was actually a voice in my head.

I tried to move again, realizing that I wasn't tied down with zip ties this time, just metal handcuffs. Judging by the lack of buzz through my veins, whatever they were pumping me full of had taken away my magic, too. So, no chance of getting those suckers off any time soon.

Which left me with one, foolproof, option: an amazing escape.

I laid still, listening to the hum of the television on the other side of the room which was showing images of world flags being burned. I didn't understand enough Ukrainian to know what was going on one way or another, however. The buzz of steps and voices on the other side of the door mingled with that of the TV, the sounds drifting from the large wooden door, and the hulking shadows of two guards that wiggled through the fogged glass on either side.

I had no idea what was waiting for me on the other side of that door, but I was going to have to make this work.

"Hello!" I yelled in what I hoped was Ukrainian, jiggling my handcuffs loudly. "I have to pee!" I jiggled again, the shadowed shapes of the guards shifting as they turned to the door. Neither of them moved to come in. What kinds of guards were these? Of course, although I knew a few phrases in Ukrainian asking to use the bathroom was pretty much it.

"Hello! I don't want to pee on the bed! I have to go!" I yelled in Czech and jiggled the cuffs again, and one of the guards stepped away. Maybe he was going to go get the keys or something. Perfect.

Honestly? I didn't actually expect that to work.

"Hello! I really have to go!" I added a bit of whine to my voice that time, jiggling the handcuffs against the metal rail with more urgency. "I have to pee."

Do you really think this is going to work?

I ignored him and instead focused on the shadow of the guard who had returned, this time joined by another. A shorter woman with a severe bun.

Damn. If that was Nastya then this was either going to be really fun, or a terrible disaster.

The door swung open. It wasn't Nastya.

It was a squat, haggard woman whose dark hair was pulled back in what turned out to be a messy bun. The guards practically threw her in before slamming the door shut and locking her in with me. The poor lady looked absolutely flustered. She gave the door a scowl before turning to me, doing her best to look professional.

"What seems to be the problem?" she asked, her eyes darting up to the top corner of my room.

A box, the same as I had seen on the train, was tacked to the wall there, directly underneath a camera that looked like it had been pulled out of a dumpster in 1989.

"I have to pee," I said, still staring at the box. "Are they watching you?"

"They watch everyone," she mumbled, shuffling over to the bed, and removing the top layer of blankets before freezing. "I don't have a key to these."

She was staring at the handcuffs now, her forehead crinkled with lines as she gave the camera one last look before she began to tuck me back in.

"But I--"

"I can't help you," she snapped, her voice harsh as she flattened the blanket over me. "I don't have the keys. You'll have to open them yourself."

"Open them myself, do I look like I have the keys?" This woman was being ridiculous. It was hard not to get frustrated with how quickly my plan was being foiled, especially with how often this woman kept glancing at the box on the wall.

"Yes." Her eyes were dark as she leaned in and placed her hand against my forehead. I was sure she wasn't taking my temperature, she was talking so low she clearly didn't want to be overheard. "They only chain the ones who know what they are doing. The dose isn't high enough. You must focus."

My heart started beating erratically, a painful pressure moving over my chest as I stared at the woman. I probably could have fought my way out of the train car, but I came here because of what Nastya said. They had Ilyan, and based on what this woman said, she knew of others like me. That meant there was a high probability she knew where he was.

I leaned closer, well I lifted my head a fraction of an inch as I fought against the straps that were over my chest. Same difference.

"Who else do they have handcuffed?" I asked, careful to keep my voice low. I didn't know if that ancient camera had a microphone, but considering this woman was playing super spy I would assume it did.

She opened her mouth to respond when the door was flung open and four guards streamed in, immediately followed by the one person I had no interest in seeing right then.

Seeing as I had threatened to rip off her head and was now handcuffed to a bed, she looked about as smug as I would expect. Things weren't looking too good for me.

"Katenka!" Nastya said with that rancid candy voice of hers, and the woman stiffened, straightening my pillow once before she turned. "What are you doing in here?"

"The guard pulled me in. She said she had to pee." Katenka actually looked like she was shaking. Apparently everyone was scared of this woman, but it didn't make me feel any better about the tightness that was assaulting my chest.

I hadn't felt this out of control since I had been taken to Edmund's camp after I first got my bite.

And you know how that ended up.

Get out of my head, old man.

"I do have to pee," I snapped, ignoring the rising panic to

face Nastya. "It's what happens when you drink water. Eat food. You have to go to the bathroom. So, a little help?"

I looked right at her, screwing my face up in all the defiant sass I could muster and shook my handcuffs.

"Leave Katenka," Nastya snapped, the woman high-tailing it out of there so fast she was a blur.

"Bye Katenka! Thanks for your help!" I called after her, wishing that there was something more I could say. Some code she could give to whoever else was in handcuffs to let them know that I was here. She was gone before I could think of anything.

Nastya didn't even turn, she just stepped forward, raising her hand in a command that sent the guards against the wall. They moved so smoothly they looked like robots, the sleek black uniforms were only enhancing that illusion. They each had a massive golden sunburst on their chest, and I half wondered that, if I tapped it, would it open up a control panel?

"Now, you gonna help me pee, then?" I asked in all my smartass glory as I turned back to Nastya, the woman still smiling.

"Why, so you can try to overpower me again?" She clicked her tongue, she actually seemed amused. At least one of us was, I was actually starting to panic.

"Well, I mean, yeah, that was the plan." Honesty was always the best policy.

"Well, let me introduce you to *my* plan." She snapped her fingers again before she turned, strutting out of the room as the guards raced to either side of me. I half expected them to unchain me and drag me out of there, but no, they just rolled me out of there, bed and all.

Okay, so this was actually working to my benefit.

I howled in feigned panic, fighting against the handcuffs as the guards led me down the hall after a still smiling Nastya.

Idiot. She clearly thought she was scaring me.

I fought harder, playing my role as I pressed against the binds, doing my best to get a good look at the hospital that was clearly doubling as a prison.

Guards were everywhere, weird guns held before them as they stood in front of every door. There weren't nearly as many nurses as I expected, but the few that I saw were all wearing the same deep green scrubs as Katenka had been. They plastered themselves to the wall and darted down halls as we moved, all of them racing as fast as they could to get out of Nastya's way.

I tried to keep track of where we were and create a map of this place in my mind, but there were simply too many turns. Too many flickering lights and cracked walls for me to be able to keep it all straight.

That was of course until we took a left turn and we all descended into hell.

The cracked and stained drywall was like a palace compared to what they had just taken me into. Broken bulbs swung on single wires, casting monster-like shadows on cement walls that dripped with blood.

I had seen this before.

I had lived this before.

Anyone else might have recoiled, frozen in panic and turned into a vegetable. Not me, this was familiar.

This was home.

I stopped fighting, there wasn't any point, because laying there, feeling all of that buzzing determination swell through my veins, I noticed there was something behind it.

The tiniest hint of my magic.

"It's okay to be scared," Nastya said from somewhere in front of us as a door swung open. "Everyone always is."

Once again she was misreading me. Whatever. If she was

going to keep underestimating me I could just use it to my advantage.

"What are you going to do with me?" I asked, letting my voice shake probably a bit more than was necessary. She didn't seem to notice.

"I'm going to have some fun." Well that was cryptic and horrifying, especially seeing as the bed I was laying on was now lifting, electric gears buzzing as I was moved to an upright position and all those straps suddenly made sense.

"I'm excited to play with my new toy," Nastya continued, grabbing two metal disks off a dented metal table, the surface so covered with rust I was amazed I recognized it as a table in the first place.

She grinned as she stepped forward. The wooden box buzzed to life and she tapped the disks together, sparks flying between them.

Oh, shit.

I really was in a mental institution, one right out of a horror story.

Nastya tapped the disks again and I cringed away, fighting against the restraints for real now as those same sparks flew between them, illuminating her face like the psychopathic doctor she was.

"What the fuck are you doing?" I snapped, still fighting against the restraints as that tiny spark of magic inside of me grew, flooding right to the tips of my fingers.

It wasn't enough to fight her, and it sure as hell wasn't enough to get me away from this mad woman. I was trapped as she placed the disks against my temples.

"I told you, I'm playing with my new toy," she crooned in a singsong voice as the electricity sparked again, but this time it went right through me.

I screamed as I shook, as my bones rattled and burned. I couldn't escape it, but part of me didn't want to.

I didn't know what she had intended to happen, but those damn disks were the shock to my system I needed to wake my magic up.

That I needed to attack her.

If only it had been enough to fight back right then. I had just one option.

I had to take it.

4

MÍRA

AND WE WERE BACK in the hospital room.

I woke up with a headache possibly worse than the one I had on the train, which made sense considering that Ms. Nasty Pants spent who knows how long running thousands of volts of electricity through me.

I was actually kinda amazed I was alive.

Actually, I probably would have died if Nastya and her little 'play time' hadn't woken my magic up. Getting electrocuted had hurt like a mother, but I forced myself to stay conscious through all of it, if only so I could keep my magic restrained.

Keep it alive.

Keep *me* alive.

My magic healed me after each bout with her machine and had continued to buzz through my veins as they wheeled my sweating, sobbing ass back to my hospital room.

And now, laying here, I could still feel it. I could already feel it rushing to my head to heal the throbbing ache from the battering it had taken.

It was just as powerful as it always was. Just as strong, even with that needle still in my arm.

I don't know what was in the medicine they were using, but it sure as hell wasn't working on me.

"We have five more countries that have reported a hostile takeover--" the voice from the TV mumbled as I blinked, focusing my magic on the button on the front of the ancient set and turning it off.

The screen popped to black, leaving the room in relative silence. I could still hear the guards outside my door talking about the same thing the reporter had, still hear the scuffing of rubber on linoleum as the haggard nurses shuffled around.

I would have to be sneaky to get out of here. But first... I scowled at the straps, letting my magic wind around them as one by one they released, handcuffs clattering to the bed, straps opening up and falling away.

If I thought my head hurt, I was mistaken. My whole body felt like it had been run through a meat grinder. This was going to make the whole tracking down Ilyan and getting out of here thing that much harder.

My magic was already rushing around my body, doing its best to heal and soothe the muscles and bones that had been attacked. But, even one step out of the bed and I fell to the floor with a clunk, my bones rattling.

Okay, I was going to need a plan B.

Today, find Ilyan. Or, maybe just figure out how to get out of the room and around the hospital without gaining the guards' attention. Seeing as there was only one door here, and I was currently wearing a blue and white hospital gown with no back, that was going to be a problem.

My body was already starting to feel a bit better, and my magic was strong enough that I was sure I could at least Stutter my way out of here. At least I hoped so. I wasn't a hundred percent sure what would happen if I failed at a Stutter, but seeing as I had just been electrocuted for a few hours, there were worse things that could happen.

I could have sworn I saw a nurses' station tucked in between halls not far from here, and if I remembered correctly the counters on those things had a lot of space underneath them. Okay, start small.

You know, and pray you don't get stuck in a wall.

Head still spinning, I closed my eyes, giving my magic one good push as I plunged myself into the nothing of a Stutter and into... a closet.

Well, at least it wasn't a wall.

The closet was lined with shelves and medical supplies, or I was sure it had been at one point. Everything in here was woefully bare. Each spot on the shelves had a label with what was supposed to be there. In some places there were only one or two things left, in others there was nothing at all.

Nasty queen or no, Ukraine had been hit as hard as everywhere else.

"I can't spare any more!" someone whisper-hissed from the other side of the door. I jumped, pulling a shield over myself and vanishing from view only seconds before the door to the closet was thrown open and two women hustled their way in.

Katenka, and someone who looked like Katenka if she had been sucked into a time machine and came out with curlier hair and freckles. It didn't take a rocket scientist to figure out what I was looking at.

"I have to try it, mom," the younger Katenka said. Called it.

"You've already used three." Katenka didn't even look at her daughter as she began checking shelves, clearly looking for something.

"I know, and before you say anything, I also know that we are running low on everything. But I can't leave him like that. I can't.

Nastya's back and you know she's going to try to remove his arm again."

"And you think keeping him asleep through that is going to make it better?" Katenka cut her off, sending the younger version of her scowling.

"She doesn't drain him as much when he's asleep. She likes to see their reaction." The young woman's face had fallen, her freckles crinkling as she wrinkled her nose. "I'm trying to keep him alive here. You know he can get us out of here. I just need to help him regain use of his magic."

Magic. *His* magic. Chances were slim it was Ilyan seeing as Katenka had said there were more than just me handcuffed and there was a high probability of more than one of them being male. But I was hopeful.

Nastya had said she liked to torture him, and this guy had clearly been tortured.

I was one second away from dropping my shield, popping back into being and demanding info when someone pounded on the door.

"Crap," the young Katenka said, pushing herself into the wall with a look of true horror on her face.

"Katenka, you in there?" a male voice nearly yelled, every syllable slurred through the wooden pane. Katenka opened it a crack, letting the man and an overwhelming smell of vodka slide in. He was old and just as haggard looking as everyone else I had seen, and had clearly been drinking.

"Sirko,." Katenka said, keeping the door open enough to talk while still blocking her daughter from view, "what do you need?"

"They need more of his blood. She's on the rampage again."

Katenka swore, waving the older man off as she moved to close the door. Giving the girl one last look.

The door had only just barely closed when the younger girl

grabbed a syringe and a bottle and escaped out to the hall. Damn. Girl was fast. I didn't even have time to consider dropping my shield that time.

I had a good feeling she had grabbed the things she said she needed, and was making her way back to this mystery man. Even if she wasn't I was going to follow her, maybe I would be able to get her alone and get information that way.

I slipped out the door before it closed, shield still in place as I prepared to weave my way through the halls after her.

Except she was gone.

Not just like swallowed into the crowd gone either. There wasn't even a crowd here to swallow her. She was just gone-gone.

I turned on the spot, taking a step one way and then another. Didn't matter which hallway I looked down, there was no one.

She had just disappeared.

I hadn't sensed any magic on her, but I hadn't really been paying attention either. There was clearly a reason why Katenka had hidden her daughter from the old man and I had an idea as to why.

She had magic. It made sense with how Katenka reacted to me. Katenka knew about magic and she was hiding her daughter, saving her from being handcuffed to a bed, too.

Damn it. Now I really needed to find her.

Before I could take another step an alarm began to go off, blue lights flashing as nurses raced into the hall and in the direction I was pretty sure my room was.

I looked down, to the needle still in my arm and the pads still on my chest. Well, I really didn't plan this one out.

"Until next time, mystery girl," I whispered before letting my magic pull me into a Stutter and back into the room where everyone clearly thought I was dead.

5

ILYAN

"I SEE YOUR MEASLY FIVE," Kaye taunted, the joy in her voice almost swallowed by the worry, "and raise you to..."

She hesitated, looking at me over the fan of her playing cards with one of her eyebrows raised so high it almost got lost in the fringe of her curly hair.

Almost.

"Ten!" She spouted the word as loud as she dared before slamming the card onto the pile on the bed between us, the metal frame jerked, sending a tremor of pain over my spine.

Her mocking taunt was replaced by maniacal laughter as she leaned back against the headboard of the rickety hospital bed that had been my prison, careful to avoid my ankle that was still locked in its restraint.

It was the only one I hadn't been able to unlock today.

Every few minutes I would try to bring up enough strength, to call on enough power, to unlock it, but it didn't budge. It couldn't break through the fog. I didn't have the strength. Nastya would be happy to know just how much she was affecting me in my months of capture. I still wasn't going to let her see.

In many ways, it didn't matter. Even with the lone restraint I was still able to shift my weight and bend my joints, which was already better than the days I couldn't unlock any and Kaye and Katenka would rub my back and joints in the hope of getting my blood to flow and the bones to heal. That was happening more frequently the longer Nastya's torturous experiments went on. Now in the third month, I was able to move freely about twice a week, if I was lucky.

Luckily, Nastya had left in a hurry a few days ago and had only returned last night. Thankfully she hadn't come for me yet, which had given me more time to heal than I usually had.

Which also meant that I got to play this ridiculous game that Kaye had created when she was five.

"Doesn't that card change the rules?" I asked, my voice slightly slurred as my tongue struggled to keep up.

Thankfully Kaye ignored it, not even a shadow of sympathy crossed her face.

"Yep! Now you are catching on." She smiled brightly and leaned over toward me, trying to sneak a peek at my cards for probably the third time in the last fifteen minutes.

"Hey!" I teased, my own laugh bursting out, only to be replaced by a wince as I tried to move my cards away from her.

The motion was too fast for my still healing shoulder, the skin still covered by one massive bruise. Although my magic was healing me, it was slower than it had been. Removing and replacing limbs would do that.

Luckily, I had been unconscious for that experiment.

"Here," Katenka whispered from beside me, her face full of the worry that Kaye was trying so hard to hide.

Her sad eyes never left mine as she handed me a styrofoam cup filled with the powdered fruit drink that had replaced orange juice in the SSU a few months ago. While it never filled the same craving that the orange juice had, I was grateful for it. I was grateful for these women, who would sneak sandwiches and Tang into my room every day. It was more than the single glass of water and bowl of liquified oatmeal the guards provided.

"I'm pretty sure looking at my cards isn't part of the rules, Kaye," I scolded, refusing to draw more attention to my shoulder than Katenka already had. "Last time we only switched two cards from each other's hands."

"Oh, yeah..." Kaye said, her voice filled with a laugh as she settled back into her spot, still glancing at me over the top of her cards. "I think I am going to change that rule. We are going to shuffle our hands and redeal them."

"You are changing a rule? Right now? I am pretty sure you can't do that." My voice was full of warning as I moved my cards away, holding them protectively. I wasn't about to give them up that easily. I had two kings, you only needed three to win the game. Unless she decided to change that rule, too. You could never be too sure with whatever Kaye had created here.

"I'm pretty sure I can," she teased right back, "I'm older than you after all."

"Appearances don't count," I teased, tucking my cards underneath my still restrained leg so she couldn't get at them. "You are only twenty-one. I am fairly certain that I am quite a bit older than you. Unless you have memories from Napoleon's journey across Europe that you would like to share."

"Immortality doesn't count then, Jan." A smug smile stretched across her face at that, two prods for the price of one.

She knew which one was going to bug me more.

"That's not my name." Her smile only grew at my growl.

"Whatever you say, Ivan."

"Not my name either," I said the words even though I knew

full well I had no way of knowing. Ivan very well could be my name, something was familiar about it.

"Denyksa?"

"No."

Katenka chuckled as she checked my blood pressure again. There was only Dr. Sirko left in this place, but from what they said he was locked in his room unless he was needed, and the poor old man had turned to drink in his solitude, the imprisonment slowly driving him mad.

This meant that Katenka was one of the few with any medical knowledge in this place, and she had taken it upon herself to make sure, to put it bluntly, that I didn't die.

"Well," Kaye said, a bright light sparking behind the worry in her eyes, "tell me when you figure it out, won't you? I'd love to meet you."

"You already have met me," I teased, all intention of playing the game gone. "I'm sitting right here."

"You know what I mean," she said, fingers fiddling with an uneven chunk of hair as she leaned back against the headboard. "Years from now you are going to show up at my door and introduce yourself clear as day and for all I know you'll be selling me vacuums, or religion, or something. I won't even know who you are!"

"Stop being so dramatic," Kaye's mother scolded, the under her breath response all-but-ignored because it happened so often.

"I'm pretty sure you will recognize me, Kaye," I said through a wince as Katenka began pressing on bones in my back and shoulder to make sure they had all healed in the right place.

She looked at me with concern, but I shook her off. Last week she had to reset my knee to get everything aligned. It was a great learning experience for Kaye, not so much for me. This pain I could take.

"You have no way of knowing that," Kaye continued, ready to continue down her assumed future. "I will be an old lady and you... you are going to look exactly the same. Probably have that same long hair you came in with."

"See," I said, my smile spreading at the corner she had backed herself into. "How could you not recognize me? If my rugged good looks never change then there is no way you will forget me, even if I am selling vacuums."

"There is no way I could forget you, anyway."

The laughter drained from the room at her words. A heavy sorrow dripped from her, infecting the air until everybody was drowning in it.

It was hard to keep the desperation out once it escaped. It was hard not to feel hopeless.

This time, however, everything felt different

Swirling over that sorrow there was a feeling of hope that I was not sure I had felt in weeks. It lined her words, it shone from her eyes.

Hope that we would escape. Hope that there was something after this and that I could knock on her door and sell her a vacuum.

"I will never forget you, Kaye," I whispered, extending my hand toward her.

Her lips turned up into a careful smile as her hand wrapped around mine, her skin warm and soft. We sat like that for a moment, eyes locked together in a million silent promises before our hands fell, the loss of contact leaving my hand feeling cold, my heart aching.

I wasn't sure if it was for her, for another, or simply for the life that would follow.

"Now," she announced as she went back to her cards as though the last few minutes hadn't happened. "Give me your cards."

"That's not a rule, Kaye," I groaned, pulling my cards out from under my leg, already knowing I didn't have another choice.

"Yes, well, if you remembered any games from your childhood we wouldn't have this problem." She smiled brightly, I glowered darkly, and Katenka just sighed, obviously not interested in revisiting this discussion with us.

"Well," Katenka began, pulling the conversation from her daughter's control, the latter just smiled brightly and leaned against the footboard. "Everything from your arm seems to be in place, although I can't attest to the internal workings. And you say you still don't have full mobility?"

I only shook my head no, I didn't really want to revisit it. Nor did I want to attempt to lift it again, the pain was almost too much.

"Well," she said with a sigh, looking away from me. It was one of her usual tells that she was about to say something uncomfortable. "Your healing has been slowing down lately. I know they were testing a new combination of drugs, to see if your..."

She stalled, and Kaye smiled knowingly.

"Magic," Kaye provided. Her mother only cringed. At least I had convinced one of them.

"...if your power can be prodded differently. But I've almost figured out the combination so we can counter it. I've been trying it on a few others here, including someone new. I should know soon if it is working."

"Thank you," I whispered as Katenka gave me one last look, the sadness in her eyes breaking my heart.

She said nothing before she was gone, the faint click of a lock sounding behind her as she spoke to the guard, their quick Ukrainian mostly indistinguishable through the heavy wood.

"Do you want to lay down now or later?" Kaye asked, the bed rattling as she moved toward me, already knowing the answer.

I only gave her a smile as she kneeled next to me, hands stable as she helped me shift and shimmy back down to my back. I tried not to wince, I tried not to let the pain show - but everything hurt. My shoulder felt like it had caught fire with even the slightest motion, an intense line of pain shooting through my bones.

I could feel my magic try to rise to meet it, try to heal it, but it was still so slow it couldn't break through whatever drug they had me on.

Sinking into the hard indentation of the mattress, the fabric settled around me like a cushion, the groan that escaped me neither from the mattress nor pain.

"I'll put the restraints back on after you fall asleep," Kaye whispered as she lay down beside me, curling up against the rail and as far from me as she could.

She had tried to curl up closer once, but everything in me had recoiled. She hadn't tried since.

"Tell me about that abbey place," she whispered, her voice barely breaking through the relaxed fog that I was drifting into. "The one where the fight was."

"Are you still trying to find it?" I asked, turning my head to look at her. I didn't even try to restrain the gasp of pain that time, it hurt that much.

"I'm always trying to find everything, Jan," she said, curling her hands underneath her chin in an effort to get comfortable. I would have offered her a pillow, but they took that away long ago. "I found Joclyn, I can find you. And then we can get you home."

"Or you could just leave without me."

She glared at the suggestion. It wasn't the first time I had mentioned it, and although she refused every time, she was slowly wearing down. She was slowly realizing, just as I was, that I wasn't a good enough reason for her and her mother to stay here.

"I know," she finally admitted, the words not hurting as much as I expected them too. "But I am not going to just leave you here unless I have no other choice. Things aren't bad enough to justify that."

"I would have to say otherwise," I said with a grunt, instantly regretting moving my arm to emphasize the point.

"They are bad to *you*, which is why I am not leaving." She placed her hand flat on the bed between us, a clear invitation for contact, to comfort, but right then I didn't need it.

I would stubbornly take everything on all on my own if it meant she would see reason and leave.

"You live in walls, Kaye," I whispered, letting my focus drift toward the ceiling.

The motion was not missed and she pulled her hand back, curling it back under her chin.

"Not for long," she said after a moment, the admission pulling my focus right to her. "Everything is in place. You know that job I got on the second floor? The one in receiving?"

She swallowed, something was there that I wasn't quite following. The drugs may make it hard to think, but it didn't make it impossible. A second too late it dawned on me just what she was saying.

"You found a way out?"

She nodded. "Once you regain control of your magic, we are getting out of here. So, no pressure, but once we are out we are going to find your Joclyn, and I am sure she is going to make the SSU pay for what they have done."

Hearing her name brought all of those memories of her right

into my mind. They slapped against my chest until my heart ached, my magic surging and pulsing until I felt it against my fingers. I lifted my hand, everything warming comfortably as a few sparks of yellow fell from me.

Kaye was already grinning. "We will be out of here sooner than you think."

6

ILYAN

HUSH NOW, child. Be still, be calm. The world will change at the new dawn. And when it does, you will see how you and I were meant to be.

Joclyn's calm voice sang through the grey halls of the hospital, the song trapped in my head as I looked toward it, expecting to see her standing there.

Sometimes she was, sometimes she wasn't. Today it was only the grey wall, the peeling paint, and splatters of blood. The image was a haunting vision against the song.

Slowly, I lifted myself from the hard floor, the residue of grime sticking to my skin.

"A když ano, uvidíte, jak jste vy a já měli být," I sang along with her in Czech as the words began to repeat, the same calm tone in the melody seeping through me as I walked toward her voice. My body moved flawlessly as the door to the hall opened before me, the twisted delusions of my dream escorting me into my house beside the beach. My dreams had brought me here so many times before, but now it was practically unrecognizable.

It was the same as the hospital.

The wide granite tiles were now cracked and broken, the large ornate paintings peeling to reveal layers of dirt and smears of red. Chandeliers swayed from the ceiling, their dripping candles flickering as they hung from strings and broken chains.

Still, she sang.

Through the rubble, through the heartbreak of my broken mind, she sang.

Her voice grew louder as I stepped through the carnage of my former mansion, tiptoeing around piles of furniture and partially burned window dressings.

"Svět se změní," I sang, my voice off key from hers as I stepped down the stairs.

As I walked. All on my own.

It was an amazing feeling, it was freedom, and even among the rubble I smiled; letting the comfort flow through me.

Heavy creaking echoed through the massive space as I made my way down the steps. For months, the sound had kept me upstairs, sure that this destruction of mind and soul was going to collapse around me.

It still could, I knew that, but it was worth the risk. If it meant true death, I would rather die here, surrounded by her voice, close to her touch, than in the prison of my reality.

"Změní v novém," I sang louder, letting my voice rattle the already unsettled structure as I yelled.

The creaking of the swaying foundation grew louder as I reached the door, the entire house heaving as I swung the burned wooden slab open to the bright sunshine and the long black hair of a beautiful woman, her voice carrying away.

"And when it does, you will see, how you and I were meant to be." Her voice was sweet, it was calm, it moved in time with the waves, it traveled on the back of the wind.

I let it fill me as I stepped away from the house and onto the wide porch. The calm, perfect beach stretched before me, the terrors of mind and reality already fading away.

"I was worried you wouldn't make it," she whispered as she placed her hand in mine, her eyes soft.

"I will always make it to you," I said, lightly tapping the tip of my finger against her nose.

She smiled at the action, even though my heart tightened at the promise I couldn't keep.

"Come." She pulled me away from the house as she began to run down the stone steps that led to the beach, the sound of the waves growing louder as they called to us.

Her laugh echoed with each step, the sound keeping time with the waves as she pulled me right into them, water splashing around our ankles.

The water was so cold against my skin that I briefly wondered where the sensation was coming from. If they had soaked me in acid again or if this was just in the dream. If this was just some unremembered piece of my memory.

"You are safe here," Joclyn whispered as she stepped before me, the cold water rising to our knees as she took my hands. "Don't go back there yet. Stay here with me."

Her silver eyes sparkled with love and light as she looked at me, as she looked into me. It was not the first time she had given me that look, and every time I saw the rare treasure it took my breath away. There was something there that I knew I had forgotten, some memory that I knew it was pulling from.

Each time I grabbed for it, I came up empty. After so many failed attempts, I no longer made the effort. I just let the love in her eyes swallow me up. I let it shield me from whatever horrors were waiting.

"Every day forever, Můj navždy," I whispered, brushing away her hair from her face as it blew in the wind, letting my hand linger against her neck, my finger circling the soft skin just below her mark. I could feel the line of rough skin, feel the bit of raised flesh, the texture sending a pleasurable ripple up my spine.

I knew better than to ask about it, to ask why she was alive and why the bite from the Vilỳ hadn't killed her. The memory was still locked in my mind, along with all the other fragments that taunted me.

Joclyn. Ovailia. Sain. Wynifred. Talon. Ryland.

Everyone but me. This one piece of vital information was still blocked from me.

Of course, I had titles. King. Krul. My lord. My love.

I heard these on repeat, but they felt wrong. As though they no longer belonged to me. As though they never had.

I had lost my name and was left only with formalities. I refused to accept that that was all I was.

It may have been a serendipitous occurrence, however. With the exception of Joclyn and Ryland, every name had been spoken aloud as Nastya played with me. Precious names that dripped from me.

Unluckily for her, she couldn't put a face to a name.

That, and based on what I had seen, I was pretty sure all of them were dead.

The thought was both joy and chilling agony and I let it shiver through me once before dispelling it into the air as I pushed it away, leaving me only to get lost in the look in her eyes.

As much as I longed for my memories, I had these moments.

In many ways that was enough.

I leaned down to kiss her, her breath brushing against my lips, only to have the calm of my paradise shattered by a scream.

My scream.

My body tensed at the noise, at the pain and tension that rippled through my bones and threatened to send me into the icy foam of the waves.

"My love," Joclyn gasped, grabbing a hold of my towering frame just before I fell.

Her arms wrapped around me, somehow holding me above the waves as they flowed around us, the motion of the water moving in time with our breaths as I inhaled their salty aroma.

I willed the fear away, I willed the pain of my body away. The respite only held for a moment before the abrasive echo of the scream brought it right back.

"I am fine," I growled, the reaction not one I would normally give her. Luckily, she didn't respond, she only held me closer, assisting me to stand as the sound came again. The scream that lived inside my head accompanied by a loud creak as the house on the hill behind us began to give way.

"Stay with me," she pleaded as she fell into me, wrapping her arms around my waist as she held herself close.

I held her against me as I cemented the feel of her in my mind. I almost wasn't fast enough.

The screams followed me out of my dreams, the same as they did every time Nastya pulled me out to this hell. My body was screaming, my chest howling as I tried to suck in air. I didn't know what she was doing to me, and I didn't care. I just held onto the dream as much as I could, clinging to it as Nastya stepped toward me, a smile on her face as she twisted that damn scalpel.

"Do you really think you will be able to find a way out of this?" she sneered as my head lulled around, as my heart ached and swelled. All I could do was moan, my screamed response muzzled by the mouthguard she had lodged in my mouth.

Of course that would make her smile more.

"You are mine and I can't wait to play." She stepped closer, but this time I didn't feel so scared. I felt angry. Enraged even, as though it would take nothing for me to just reach forward and end her.

I wanted to. I needed to.

Except those feelings didn't seem the same as they usually did. They felt stronger. Almost like they didn't belong to me.

I didn't have any time to think about it before her twisted smile spread and the scalpel plunged into my arm, pain spreading through me as I was ripped apart and I forced myself out of this reality and into another one.

One where I could only hope that those feelings had come from.

One with her.

7

RYLAND

I COULDN'T SLEEP.

Although it wasn't without trying. I had been awake for days and now I was stuck in a tossing and turning hell, forced to watch the hours tick down on the old alarm clock on my nightstand.

The one Mira found early on in the fall of society and fixed for me so I wouldn't be late to my training sessions with her.

I was sure the fact that she was the one who had given it to me was contributing to my lack of sleep.

We were leaving in just a few hours, now.

Then she would be home and I would keep her safe.

"Fucking hell." I grabbed my pillow, throwing it over my face as I smothered the scream and the long line of expletives that came after.

This was getting ridiculous. I needed to stop pretending she didn't matter to me. Stop pretending she was--

I cut my thoughts off with a groan, practically throwing myself out of bed and into the bathroom. There was no way in hell I was getting any sleep, so I might as well get ready.

A quick shower later and I was pulling on my dark jeans and throwing the last of the things I was going to need in my bag.

It was only after I was dressed, packed, and out of my room that I realized the absolute ridiculousness of what I was doing. I now, officially, had nowhere to go and nothing to do for the next few hours. At least tossing in bed I had something.

"Mother--" I snarled, and almost turned right back around to throw myself in my bed to stare at that damn alarm clock when I froze, hand still on the knob.

There was something I needed to get. If we were going to rescue Míra, and she had been kidnapped and beaten and who knows what else, she was going to need clothes. I could get her clothes.

I had walked the halls to Míra's room so many times over the years that I didn't even look up. I just stared at the floor, trying to ignore the way my heart grew louder and louder in my ears with each step.

It didn't get any better when I opened the door.

Everything about her room was wrong.

But not wrong in that she wasn't there, or that it had been ransacked by some thief looking for something. Actually, I think I would have been less worried if her room had been ransacked. But no, it was clean. For Míra, that was more than a little unusual.

Everything was in its place, the blanket folded on the chair, laundry put away, even her pillow had been fluffed. It looked like a museum, all except for the square of paper in the middle of the bed.

My bag dropped to the ground with thud as I practically threw myself it, grabbing the paper that was emblazoned with the curly writing that she always used.

RYLAND

She had left a note. She was an overdramatic sixteen year old, of course she had left a note.

I may have opened the letter a bit too eagerly, seeing as I ripped the damn thing in half. Still better than burning it, at least I could still read it.

RY-

Surprise! I followed you to London! Of course, you already know that if you are reading this. Although if you are reading this that means things probably didn't go as well as I was hoping and I didn't make it back.

Leave it to me to survive all the crap in the world and die while saving your ass, because I am one hundred percent sure that if I die, that's how I am going down.

I SMILED, THE GRIN PULLING PAINFULLY AT MY FACE AND THE stupid tears that were pouring from my eyes. It shouldn't be funny, that little bugger shouldn't have been right.

NOW, DON'T BE MAD AT ME FOR GOING, AND REALLY DON'T BE MAD AT *me for dying. But I had to, I had to prove that I was capable of doing all those things you seem to think I am too young for. I am just as strong as you, Ryland.*

I want to be.

Because I want to be with you. Because I love you.

I WAS BARELY ABLE TO HOLD ONTO THE PAPER, MY HANDS WERE shaking so much. I tried to sit down but promptly missed the bed and slid down right to the floor. I didn't even try to get back up, I was too focused on her note. My heart was beating too fast, anyway.

THERE, I SAID IT, MY DEATH BED CONFESSION. I'VE BEEN IN LOVE WITH you for a while, and I know I shouldn't because you are soooooo much older than me (newsflash, five years is not that long). But it doesn't matter because we are going to live forever, well, I guess you are now. But I had to show you that I'm not a child anymore.

Maybe I had to prove it to me, too.

So, there it is. I'm probably dead, and I really am sorry because I really wanted to kiss you.

Love you.

Míra.

I JUST STARED AT THE LETTER, AND HER SWIRLY WRITING AND THE few marks from teardrops on the paper that might have come from either her or me. After a few minutes my heart rate began to slow, even though I didn't feel like I was calming down.

Everything felt like it was speeding up.

"Any reason you are sitting on Míra's bed?"

I jumped up so fast I slammed my knee into her footboard, sending searing pain up and down my leg.

"Mother--" Thank God my magic was already healing me or that would have made the rescue mission interesting. "What are you doing sneaking up on people, Thom?"

"What are you doing sitting on Míra's bed, Ryland?" Thom mocked my frustration as he stepped into the room, pulling himself out of the shadowed hall and into the dimly lit space.

He looked just as exhausted as I felt. He had dark rings under his eyes, and was wearing pajamas that looked both too big and too small. And one sock.

"Are you sleepwalking?" I chuckled, looking him up and down as he nodded.

"What?" He froze, following my gaze to the one sock situation. "No. Wyn wanted some candy that Mira stores in here. She asks. I jump."

"And you were worried about why I was sitting on her floor? You're stealing." Thom just shrugged at me and went back to the dresser which he promptly began going through.

"Have you ever told Wyn 'no'?" That was really all he needed to ask.

"Once. I regretted it."

"Exactly." He yawned and opened another drawer, clearly not interested in taking more than a cursory glance. "Besides, it looks like you are snooping too."

He eyed the two halves of the letter in my hand before yawning again and opening yet another drawer.

"It was addressed to me." I showed him the front, careful to keep all of the loopy writing on the inside hidden.

"Oh, so a love letter then?"

"No." I answered way too fast and I knew it. My brother froze, snickering as he turned to face me, a bag of pilfered candy in his hands.

"No? Could you sound any more guilty, Ryland." Thom didn't even give me a chance to react before he waved his hand and the two halves of the letter flew out from between my fingers and right into his.

"Give it back, Thom. We don't have to be children about this." My heart had sped up again, but now it was for a whole different reason. I jumped up, intent to get them back.

"Oh, I think we do. Besides, I missed pestering you as a child, this may be my only opportunity." He grinned at me, popping a few pieces of the candy in his mouth before he began to read. His eyes grew big almost immediately. "Damn."

I had never felt this nervous about anything. Ever.

"Now will you give it back?" I snapped, reaching for the letter again, but Thom just grabbed the candy bag and sat himself on the bed.

"Correct me if I'm wrong, but I'm pretty sure that girl loves you." Thom handed the letter to me and I snatched it back, sitting on the bed next to him, before he had a chance to change his mind.

"You think?"

"I mean, she--"

"I know, Thom," I cut him off, stealing a few pieces of candy. "She made that clear enough when she saved my ass. I probably didn't need the letter. I would have known anyway."

Thom instantly began to snicker, but cut it off quickly when I let one spark of my magic flare from the tips of my fingers.

"You love her, too." It wasn't a question, and it wasn't full of any of the sass that I would usually get from him. Just honesty. Just understanding.

I nodded. "Her magic sparked against mine in the hospital in Prague. But I was with Risha... and then Míra killed Risha. It's complicated." The last words were more of a snarl. Complicated was probably an understatement for how Míra made me feel. Frustrated. Worried. Angry. Passionate in every way. It made for a firestorm of emotions.

"But I do care about her," I said after a minute, everything calming at the admission.

"Your raging need to go save her is suddenly making sense." Thom tilted the bag of candy to me and I took more than a few. Candy was about as rare as everything else in this world. Both Míra and Wyn would probably be upset we were eating it all.

"I just need her to be safe." Just saying it seemed to ignite something inside of me.

"So love it is then. It's how you know. You want to keep them safe. Even if it means going to get them candy at four in the morning and risking their wrath when you eat it all so you can help your brother." Thom gave me a grin, dreads swinging as he titled the bag into his mouth and promptly emptied it. "You've got it bad, bro. And seeing as she literally risked her life to save you, so does she."

He stood, tossing the bag into the garbage can that was empty for probably the first time I'd been in here.

"Doesn't change the fact that she is, in fact, younger than me." I said the same thing I had been telling myself for years, but after reading her letter it seemed like a flimsy excuse. No, it *was* a flimsy excuse.

"Spoken like a mortal. Get over yourself Ryland. She's right. In fifty years it won't even matter. Your magic has found its match, and I've seen you two together enough to know you have too. Now, if you excuse me, I need to go rub my empress's feet and beg for forgiveness." Thom clapped me on the shoulder, grinning broadly as he winked and strutted his way out of the room, looking like a conquering hero, with one sock. The look was even more dramatic thanks to his swinging dreads.

I just stared at him for a while, the paper still clutched in my hand as I laid back on her bed, and my eyes finally drifted closed.

"I'm coming, Míra."

8

JOCLYN

"Do you really think you will be able to find a way out of this?" The woman's voice echoed over the stone walls, the sweet acidity of her laugh toxic as I lifted my head, staring right at the same blonde woman that I had seen in the tent.

The one who had been talking about Ilyan.

Now, she stood feet away from me, twisting a scalpel with a blood stained blade between her fingers.

A noise echoed from behind me, the sounds muffled and panicked as the woman approached. Her smile spread with each step.

I tried to see where the noise was coming from, to see what that nasty woman with the scalpel was smiling at. But I couldn't, my focus was locked on the woman.

A woman who approached me, except it wasn't me she was approaching. And I wasn't there.

It wasn't a dream either, no matter how clear it was. The clear images could only mean one thing. This was a sight and what I was seeing was happening right then.

The muffled sounds of a voice echoed in my ears again, the

woman only steps away as she lifted the blade, letting it catch the dim light of the room.

There was only a single bulb hung far overhead, but it was enough to illuminate the horrors of this place. Blood streaked walls, dented metal tables covered in rusty medical tools, a cracked mirror. It truly was something out of a horror movie.

I didn't want to be there, and I certainly didn't want to see what came next, not that I had a choice.

"You are mine, and I can't wait to play." The muffled voice turned into a scream as the scalpel lowered to a scarred arm, and the light overhead began to flicker.

Pain raced over everything, electricity sparking as the world went in and out of focus and whoever she was torturing was reflected back at me through the mirror.

"Ilyan!" I sat straight up in bed, springs creaking as steps echoed down the hall on the other side of the door I had magicked out of existence.

Great.

I had fallen asleep in the Tõuha, drifted off while swimming in the waves with Ilyan, something which wasn't out of the ordinary for me. Waking up screaming from dreams of sight was new, however. Seeing as I had shielded this room's existence from the world, it was no surprise people were running through the halls outside it in a panic.

St. Vitus Cathedral and all the outbuildings had been a construction zone for months. It was still worth the risk to come here, if only to sleep in the room Ilyan and I had shared and drift to sleep in his arms inside the Tõuha. But it looked like my welcome had officially run out.

Wiping the sweat from my brow, I grabbed my phone and slipped into the bathroom, determined to steal a quick shower before Ry and I headed to Kiev.

One look at my phone, however, and those plans had to change.

I had slept through the alarm I set.

It was almost seven a.m. and I had five missed calls. Three from Ryland, Two from Wyn, and one text message that said: 'We are saving your husband. Get your ass down here.'

My heart skipped a beat at that. Ilyan. I was going to see Ilyan today.

Although, after that dream I was starting to worry about what shape he would be in.

I had fallen asleep in the Tŏuha, meaning that whatever connection I had with Ilyan was still there, that very well could have been him in that room with that... that...

"Bitch." I spat before brushing my teeth with a new found fury. "I'm going to stab her with a scalpel and see how she likes it."

I spat the rest of the toothpaste out, quickly pulling my hair up as yet another text message came in.

'Ryland is going to go without you if you are not here soon.'

'Go spank a fish, I'll be right there.' I stared at the message. Spank a fish? That was not what I meant to send, but a lucky combination of sleepy typing and autocorrect may have worked in my favor.

I sent it anyway.

Her reply was instantaneous. 'Spank a fish?'

Okay, that time I laughed. I laughed like I hadn't in years, and it felt good. Really good. Even with the horrifying images that had woken me up, I was on cloud nine. We knew where Ilyan was, and today I was going to get him.

Teeth brushed, I pulled the old earthen mug off the back of the toilet, covering it with my hand to refill it with the honey scented Black Water. Normally, it was just food, but today I needed to see.

The rescue mission today was either going to work, or it wasn't, and any insight I could get that didn't involve scalpels and flashing lights was wanted.

"Please let him be okay," I mumbled before I took a drink, letting the water fill me and ignite my magic. The warm water flooded through every inch of me, my head spinning as the Drak magic ignited and pulled me right into sight.

Everything went black before lights began to flash in a light and dark strobe, speeding up as the pulse of a heart turned erratic. The thunderous beat faded as the lights did, leaving us looking at the massive army Ryland and I had found in a clearing, the huddled masses drilled and fought around a cluster of tents, all of them ready for battle. They marched past my sight as it began to fade to the hospital, the large cement building set in the middle of the city. I moved through the halls, the same flashing lights returning before everything went black and the sight left.

There was nothing new here. Which should be a good thing. Hopefully we were on the right track.

I took another drink of the Black Water, turning toward the room where the shouts from the hallway had grown. I didn't wait around to see if they were going to break down the wall, though.

This place was sacred to me, and I knew it was only a matter of time before they found it. It would figure that they would find it today.

Running my hands over the old dresser, I took one last look at the room before I stepped forward and into a Stutter.

The world compressed around me, pressing so hard that I swear I could feel my soul. I didn't dare breathe for fear my lungs would explode as I stepped into the void between worlds and the swirling ribbons of color and time that surrounded me.

Flashes of my life, of a hundred lives, weaved around me in a dance, everything moving so fast that I was sure even if I reached out to grab one of the beautiful ribbons it would just slip between my fingers.

In the time it took me to take one step, however, it was gone. The room in Prague was gone and I was back in the caves of Imdalind, standing in the center of the main entrance hall and in front of three of the best people I knew.

"I will have you know, I spanked a fish, Jos!" Wyn called to me as she rushed over, Thom and Ryland right on her heels. She was possibly the only one out of the three that looked even half awake. Thom looked like he had been hit by a truck, and Ryland looked like he had been run over by one a few times.

The rings underneath his eyes were so dark that they nearly matched the black of his curly hair.

"What happened to you?" I probably sounded more accusatory than I should have, but he looked like hell. "You sure you are up for this?"

"What?" Ryland mumbled, his brain taking more than a second to catch up. "No! Yes! I'm fine. I'm ready. I just... I slept in too."

There was something else there, especially with how Thom was smiling, his dreads swinging as he rocked on his toes.

"Do I want to know?"

"No!" Ryland yelled, the same second that Wyn and Thom both grinned and said "Yes!" Ryland instantly turned on Thom.

"You told her?"

Poor guy looked like a jungle cat waiting to strike. I might have been scared of the look he was giving them, but he wasn't looking at me, and Wyn actually looked scared for her life. That was rare enough that I was just going to sit back and enjoy the show. I took a drink from my mug.

"He tells me everything." Wyn leaned in, her eyes blazing as she faced him. I was fairly certain the temperature of the hall increased five degrees.

"Well, he shouldn't have told you this!" Ryland spat, sparks drifting from his fingers as fire raged from hers.

What the hell? Talk about going from zero to a hundred. We were all cranky this morning.

"Can we please not tear down the hall?" I asked, fully aware I was groaning. Sleep deprived Ryland was not someone you wanted to double-cross, and I was starting to realize that pregnant Wyn was just as bad. If she kept this up she was going to have to let more than me and Thom in on her secret.

"I was going to burn it down, not tear it down," Wyn said playfully, even though she and Ryland were still glaring at each other.

"Whatever. It's too early for this, you can tell me whatever nonsense you are fighting over later. Besides, we have bigger things to be doing." That got everyone's attention. They all turned to me, eyes as bright and hopeful as the bubble that had lived in my chest for the last twelve hours.

"Like spank a fish?" Thom asked with a yawn. No one even reacted.

I finished my water, handing Wyn my mug, who took it without question, even if Thom was looking at it with murderous intent.

"Tell you what, Thom. You can spank a fish with Ilyan when we bring him home," I said, holding out my hand to Ryland who sneered at it for a second before he took it.

Thom may have been afraid of Black Water, but Ryland was terrified of a Stutter.

"Sounds like the weirdest welcome home celebration I've ever been to. I'm in." I never thought I would see Thom so happy about a fish spanking party. But then again, I was grinning just as big and I was the one who had suggested it.

"Be quick. Be safe. We'll hold down the fort," Wyn said, and I gave her a nod before my magic swelled and pulled us right into the Stutter.

Everything was electrified with where we were going, my mind buzzing as I thought of that hospital and the hill that Ryland had pointed out on the map to me before.

I barely even looked at the quick moving ribbons, the flashes of color slowing into something that I could have sworn was an image.

An image of Ovailia on a train. The same one I had seen in my sight. I turned to look, but before I could everything sped back up, the images turning to ribbons of color before the world rematerialized before us.

Ryland was already on his knees, vomiting out the contents of his stomach. I stood on top of a building, the wind whipping my hair around my face as I stared down at the hospital.

The same hospital I had seen in my sight.

Surrounded by the army that I hadn't.

The Kyō were already here.

9

WYN

I ALWAYS HATED when Joclyn left me and Thom in charge.

It didn't happen often, but when it did things always seemed to go awry. People would get into weird gambling rings, the kids would use their magic in ways they weren't supposed to, and something would inevitably blow up.

It didn't matter that either Thom or I were probably behind all of it, that was just another sign that we really weren't meant to lead. Especially a group as big as this.

Chosen from all over the globe had been streaming into Imdalind, led by the Skříteks that used to call this place home. It wasn't until the fifth group had arrived from the US that I realized just how much of the caves I hadn't been able to clear out. We were officially busting out of the seams.

Which was why I had snuck off to my room about an hour ago after finding room in one of the caves for the fifty people who had just shown up, leaving Etma in charge for 'just a few minutes'.

I needed to breathe. And I needed to settle my stomach. It was getting harder and harder to hide this pregnancy.

I hadn't been anywhere near this sick with Rosaline.

My stomach twisted again and I rolled over, scowling at the hard crackers that were supposed to settle my stomach and had instead made it worse.

I had no sooner turned over when the door flew open, a cloud of black smoke billowing in like a monster ready to devour everything in its path. Screaming, I sat straight up, magic already rushing through the bed and the stone as I searched for whoever was attacking us. Whatever bastard thought they could get past me was going to find themselves burned to a crisp.

A body rushed in through the black and I jumped to my feet, hands out as I faced blue eyes amongst the pool of black, coils of hair down his back.

Thom.

"What happened, are we under attack?" I snapped, hands still out as fire sparked from each of my fingertips. I probably looked like a human candelabra amidst the black smoke that had sucked all the light from the room.

"Nope. Everything is fine." Thom shook his head and closed the door, leaving us trapped with the smoke.

"Fine, then what the hell are you doing?" I kept my hands up, still warning him of the trouble he had walked into.

Never disturb a pregnant lady when she is getting some much needed rest.

"Running." Thom rushed away from the door, some of the smoke finally falling away so I could see him properly. Not that he looked much different now when not surrounded by the swirls of black smoke. He was smothered, head to toe, in ash.

"Running? Do I need to ask from whom?"

"Kids. I *might* have made them think I was the ghost of Edmund, come to kill them all." He was clearly trying to disguise a laugh as he danced beside the door, cracking the door to peer out as the sound of dozens of tiny feet ran through the hall, a few voices filtering through.

"You guys go that way. We can cut him off."

"How do you cut him off? He's a ghost?"

"Why are we hunting a ghost?"

And then they were gone, leaving Thom grinning as he closed the door, then sliding down it to the floor as he laughed.

"You do realize that you essentially turned a whole bunch of children, with magic, into ghost hunters, right?" I asked, sitting down on the foot of the bed and grabbing another one of the crackers. My stomach turned just from having it in my hand. This was not going to end well.

Maybe I should just go camp out in the bathroom again.

"That's what's so great about it. It'll keep them busy." Thom jumped to his feet, stripping off his shirt and revealing the olive skin beneath. He was so covered in black soot that he almost looked like a floating torso.

"And you'll be able to tease them whenever you feel like it?" I asked, knowing him too well. "Well, we both can," he said with a smile. "I know you won't turn down an opportunity to terrorize little children. Plus, it would be super fun if we could make the ghost of Edmund breathe fire."

I laughed, he knew me too well too.

"Alright. I'm in. Although, at the rate I am going I will be breathing puke not fire." My stomach spun again and Thom's face fell.

"Still bad?" I nodded in answer and I laid back on the bed.

"I'm a badass assassin, Thom. And I just want to assassinate a toilet." Damn it! Just thinking of the toilet was bringing all of that swirling nausea back into existence.

"You do know you can't assassinate a toilet, right," Thom said, crawling over the bed to lay beside me. He left a wide black strip of whatever he had covered himself with behind, staining the red sheet black.

If it didn't look so cool, and if I didn't feel ready to add vomit to the contemporary art, I might have cared.

"Do you want to watch me assassinate a toilet? Because I will, just to prove you wrong."

"Nah." Thom wrapped his hand around mine as we both laid there, that mischievous grin of his coming back. "I'll just tell the kids that's where the ghost is. They'll do it for you."

"But then how will I vomit my guts up while I grow your tiny uterus demon?"

"Demon, eh?" Thom propped himself up on his elbow, leaning over me as the hand wrapped around mine moved to trace the bottom of the Styx shirt I was wearing. "And here I was thinking it was a baby. Hello little demon, I'm your daddy. I can't wait for you to claw your way out of your mommy's belly--"

"Thom," I half-pleaded, half-laughed. I was trying not to puke all over the bed but the images he was conjuring were not helping with the whole not vomiting thing.

Unfortunately, he just ignored me.

"I'm going to teach you how to possess bodies and raise the dead and rule the underworld--"

"Are we trying to bring another Sain into the world?" I asked, and that shut him up.

"Naw, but that man was a demon. Maybe that's what Black Water is, an elixir of souls harvested from hell. Don't tell Jos I said that," He added quickly, his blue eyes bright even as he laughed.

I just rolled my eyes. Sometimes I could have sworn that he was more scared of Black Water than he ever had been of Edmund.

"You know you gotta get over your fear of that stuff, right?"

"Maybe in another hundred years. You do know it burns right?" His voice shook, and I couldn't help it. I laughed.

"Is the big bad ghost of Edmund scared of a little burn?" I

tried to pat his head, really drive the taunt home, but he batted my hand away, his face all serious now.

"Well, that and someone else seeing into my future. I'd rather not know when bad stuff is coming." His voice cracked. We had talked about this before, we had talked about all of it, but there was something broken there. Something that was cracking in his eyes as his fingers stopped tracing and he instead flattened his hand against my stomach, which thankfully hadn't developed more than a 'I ate too many tacos for dinner' bump.

"I have a feeling that good stuff is coming." I placed my hand over his, letting my magic move through him in a warm wave. His magic perked up, moving right to mine as it always did. As it had every day since our bonding. My perfect match.

God, I loved him.

"You say that, but you do realize that Jos is heading into a war zone to rescue my brother and every Chosen in the world is heading for us so some evil tyrants don't harvest them for electricity, right?"

"Way to suck the joy out of the room, Thom." I rolled my eyes at him again, making sure to over exaggerate the motion. He hated that.

"I'm being realistic, Wyn." He narrowed his eyes at me. Damn, he was all business now.

"So am I." He tried to pull away, but I gripped his hand, my magic still flooding through him as I pressed his palm to my stomach. "Listen to me and your uterus demon spawn."

He tried to pull away again, but I held on tight, staring him down as I let my magic grow.

His power was a warm rain against my fire, the two the perfect combination as I let them twist together in that line of power that was so distinctly ours; then I pushed it inside me. I prodded our magic through his hand, through me, and right into the child Thom and I created.

So tiny. So precious.

Just as precious as the wisp of smoke that was their magic.

Not their magic.

His magic.

Thom felt it as I did, his eyes widening as he looked at me. He didn't even try to hide his tears.

"It's a boy?"

I nodded and he tackled me, his lips pressing against mine in a hunger that flooded me. The fire that lived in my soul ignited and I wrapped my arms around him. Suddenly the twist of nausea in my stomach didn't matter.

I wanted Thom. I wanted him everywhere.

I had only just hooked my fingers under the waistband of his pants when someone knocked on the door with so much urgency that you would think the ghost of Edmund *had* come back.

"Edmund is dead, there is no ghost, we're busy!" Thom yelled toward the door before coming back to kiss me. His mind was obviously in the same place mine was.

"What?" a voice shouted through the door.

"Come back later!" Thom and I yelled together before turning back to yet more kissing. Why did he have to taste so good?

"I can't! We're under attack!" We both froze, this didn't sound like a ghost story. "That woman! Her magic is alive. She's trying to kill us all!"

10

WYN

AT LEAST THOM and I hadn't caused the chaos this time, not that that was saying much.

Bangs and blasts echoed from the large room we had been using as the hospital wing, the stone of the cave groaning as whatever attacks she was using blasted against it.

"You know, I'm gonna be pissed if she brings anything down." I had worked too damn hard to get this cave back into a suitable living condition to just let some renegade bring it all down.

"Well, that's the last thing I want," Thom said with a bark, he was already going into full takedown mode. "You distract her, I'll restrain her from behind."

"Why do I have to be the distraction?" I snapped as we rounded the corner and another blast rattled over the stone.

"Because then you can use your magic. Unless you want to be the one to go in 'all stealthy'?" He grinned at me, already victorious. He knew I wasn't going to agree to that, and that earned him a scowl.

"Hell no."

"That's my girl."

Insufferable man.

Thom blew me a kiss before he vanished from sight, his magic pulsing through the air as he sped ahead of me.

I guess I would need to hurry if I wanted to have any kind of fun.

I kept close to the rumbling of Thom's magic as we raced through the last stretch of hall and toward the hospital wing that blast after blast was echoing from. The hallway was lined with a myriad of patients, kids, and Chosen who were all peeking in like this was some kind of training exercise and not a crazed woman trying to finish her task to capture The Oheň.

I didn't care what anyone said, I was still disappointed I didn't get a cool nickname.

"Please! If you will just listen to us," one of the Skříteks yelled, Giel, judging by the firm command of the voice. Giel had never been one to back away from a fight.

"Sorry, there's no point in talking anymore," the woman returned, followed by another flash of light.

I slowed to a walk, putting as much of a strut into my step as I could as Thom and I weaved through the crowd and into the room, leaving more than one confused Chosen behind as an invisible Thom pushed them aside.

Sure enough, Giel, stood before about five other Skříteks, all of them standing calmly behind a shield as they tried to reason with the woman Ryland had captured a week ago.

She tried to kill him in an attempt to get to Joclyn, but her magic was still that stringy rotten stuff that Edmund's Vilỳs gave off. As powerful as that magic was, it couldn't compete with the pure, healed, magic of the Chosen. As a thank you for her attempted murder, Joclyn had healed, but not centered, the woman's magic so that she couldn't use it. Somehow she had found a way to use her busted magic regardless. Not that the poor girl knew what she was doing.

And here I was thinking that she was in here killing everyone. At least this wouldn't take too long.

"Hi! Can I join the party?" I asked loudly, putting a stick of gum in my mouth as I walked the rest of the way in. Everyone's focus pulled to me. Giel gave me a smile and a sigh, clearly happy for the backup.

The woman, however, screamed and sent what she clearly thought was her biggest and best attack my way. I just feigned a yawn and swiped my hand, sending it uselessly into the same shield that Giel and the others had erected to protect themselves.

"What have you done to my magic?" the woman screamed, sending another attack, which I again sent to the side.

"I, personally, haven't done anything. But you seem to be catching on quick." Another attack, and another deflection. I had to hand it to her. With no training, and only having used that diseased magic before now, she was actually doing pretty well.

I mean, she wasn't going to be able to go up against me, but I didn't need to rub that in quite yet. Not that I had taken it off the table.

"What have you done to my magic?" she asked again. I was supposed to be distracting her, yes, but I was all geared up to fight not chit-chat.

"It's fixed." I grinned at her, holding my hand out as I pulled at the magic that was typical for a Trpaslík and not the fire magic that was so unique to me. It crackled on my palm before I sent it into the air in an arc, the power visible as I lifted one of the many hospital beds and spun it around in the air like it was on the point of a top.

She stared at it, unable to disguise her awe at the power.

Who would have thought a simple spinning bed would work so well as a distraction. Thom had gotten nearly all the way behind her without her noticing and I had spread my fire magic through the stone of the floor, letting it pool right beneath her feet. I was sure she could feel the heat of it with how she shifted her weight, even if she didn't know what it was.

One step out of line and I was going to sink her in a pool of lava. And there went my stomach, just the reminder of the smell of burning flesh wasn't exactly helping with the whole 'don't vomit on the bad girl' situation. How the hell had I killed so many people when I was pregnant with Rosaline? Maybe morning sickness was worse with boys...

"You think I care about that?" she snapped, pulling me out of my reverie as I stared at her, the bed still spinning between us even though she clearly wasn't paying attention to it anymore. She was back to snarling at me.

I grinned at her, my magic still heating below her as I felt Thom's magic position right behind her.

"No, but all it was supposed to do was distract you anyway." I shrugged, and Thom reacted, his hand flinging out as magical ropes of glittering orange spread from him, wrapping around her like a maiden tied to railroad tracks.

"Well that was--" Thom began, only to be flung aside as his ropes exploded, the woman smashing her way out with a scream.

She turned to me, eyes enraged, back arched, she was even baring her teeth like some kind of dog as she heaved. I was sure she saw it as a threat. With how much magic she was letting grow in her palms I actually had a brief moment of thinking that she might be able to do some real damage. It might have been a good fight, but I was too sick to care.

I shrugged and threw the spinning bed at her.

It slammed into her as she screamed, Giel and the others

that were watching from behind the shield and from the doorway gasping as both bed and woman were slammed into the wall.

"What the hell was that, Wyn?" Thom asked with half a laugh as he popped back into existence.

"It was me not using rope and avoiding the smell of human flesh burning." My stomach heaved, but I clenched my jaw, forcing it to behave. "You're welcome."

Thom rolled his eyes at me as we both raced to the bed and the woman who was groaning and trying to pick herself back up.

"Next time, chains." I said, letting my magic wind around her before she was able to pull herself to standing.

"Do you really think that will stop me?" she snarled, already trying to pull her magic to her hands.

"Yes." I leaned in, smiling as I flicked a little bit of my magic to life and the chains caught fire. "I have all the ways to stop you."

I wasn't sure she heard that last part though, considering she was screaming from the fire. So much for avoiding the smell of human flesh.

"Oh god," I grumbled, snapping my jaw shut the second Thom looked at me.

"Wyn. Watch it."

Keeping my face as far from 'I am not going to vomit' as possible I pulled the fire back into me, leaving her clothes a bit scorched even as her magic repaired the burns on her skin.

"You really don't want to try me." For once, the woman actually seemed scared.

She sat there, covered in chains, huddled next to the remains of the bed I had thrown at her head, and she actually nodded. I resisted the urge to give into my smug celebration, even if Thom rolled his eyes at me. He knew that I would be rubbing in this victory later.

"Okay, awesome." I sat straight up, waving to Giel and the others as I set the bed nearest me upright, letting my magic pick up the now restrained woman and plop her right back onto the squishy mattress.

"So now that we got all of that out of our system." I leaned against the bed frame, sitting myself right next to the woman who was clearly trying to find a way out of the chains. Again. "Are you going to tell me what you know about the SSU, now?"

"Like I'd ever tell you that," she said with enough malice that I was sure she would have spat at me if she wasn't afraid I would burn her. I did anyway. It didn't take more than a pulse of power to light the chains on fire with a greater intensity than before.

"Wyn." Thom's reminder was a calm wave and I shut the flames off.

"I think you will. See, the Queen and I have different ideas of torture and seeing as the Queen left me in charge--" I let the threat hang as I shrugged, feeling my magic boil in excitement as it flooded the chains again. I didn't let them catch fire, I just let them heat until she began to sweat.

"So... tell me about the SSU. About this 'God'," I made sure to give the word air quotes, "that they have."

"I will never--"

"Yes, we know," Thom grumbled from above me. "You will never tell us. Except that the Kyō have now taken over the world and the SSU will fall any day. You aren't protecting anyone."

"You're lying."

"Why is it always the revolutionaries that are so stubborn?" I mumbled, pulling out my phone and tapping on my screen as the woman continued to snarl at me. "Here."

Turning my phone to her, she gave me one last glare before

looking at the headlines. I scrolled through them, the list of countries that fell going on and on and on.

"You're... you're lying!" she was snarling, even if she still didn't seem so convinced. She didn't even try to fight against the chains. She just sat in the bed, looking like a caged jungle cat.

"Yes, because I enjoy wasting my time creating hundreds of fake news articles." I rolled my eyes and turned to Thom, who was still scowling at the woman.

His magic warmed as I turned to him. I hadn't realized how much he was shielding me. He wasn't letting anyone touch me or his uterus demon. I would have to scold him for being overprotective later; that was if seeing how he took care of me wasn't such a turn on.

What the hell pregnancy hormones? Getting turned on by a protective guy while I'm seconds away from torturing this woman. At least I didn't want to throw up anymore.

"The SSU is going to fall. Our Queen went to help." It was a lie, but it did what I needed it to do and she snarled at me again. "She is going to find the woman who leads you and end the SSU once and for all."

Another lie, but I didn't care, neither did the woman who went from snarling to laughing.

"You think she can defeat Nastya Klotz? You are all fools. Leader Klotz is the greatest ruler Ukraine has ever known, and with her God--" She laughed again, but I just stood there, pretending to look horrified as the information that I wanted anyway came pouring out of the woman's mouth. "She wants your 'Queen'. And now your queen is going right to her, to find the man she took. She's been playing with him for years, you know. I've heard his screams. Nastya defeated him and she will defeat your Queen as well."

Oh, the pride of a revolutionary. That was just too easy.

"Oh no!" I gasped, not even trying to make it sound like real shock. "Do you mean The Oheň is walking into a trap? Heaven save us!" I turned in feigned shock to Thom who was already tapping on his cell phone screen, probably sending Jos a text message.

When I turned back, the woman just stared at me in shock, realizing what she had done, and what she'd walked into.

"What did you--" she began, already yelling.

"Thanks for all your help," I sassed, patting her on the knee before I tightened the chains, moving them over her mouth so she didn't drive everyone in the hospital mad. "And no, since I know you are going to ask, I didn't give you anything. I've just been around a few too many revolutions to know how to get information. Although, burning would have been fun too."

I grinned at her, finally pulling my fire magic back as Giel raced over, adding her own binds to the woman. The bound woman screamed as Thom and I walked away. I couldn't make out much through the chains, but I was one hundred percent sure there were more than a few expletives thrown my way.

"You know, you are ruthless," Thom hissed in my ear as we left the infirmary, hand already around my waist as he pulled me against him.

"Well, she interrupted something I really wanted. I wasn't going to let that slide." I wound my arm around his waist, sticking my hand in his back pocket and squeezing with enough force that he jumped.

"I take it we are continuing where we left off?" His voice was a low rumble as he nipped at my earlobe, the tiniest hint of his French accent peeking through as it always did when he was turned on or angry.

"Oh no," I teased, turning us into the hall that Jos and Ilyan's rooms were in. "I'm going to get what I want. And I'm going to remind you just how strong your mate is. Just how much she takes what she wants."

"Yes, please." Thom grinned as I opened the door to Jos's room and threw him in, shutting the door behind him.

"I'm going to go take a nap!" I yelled, turning back to our room and racing down the hall. Knowing he was going to follow.

And that I wouldn't be sleeping.

11

ILYAN

IT WAS the screams that woke me.

The same as they did every morning. As they did every moment someone walked into the hallway we were all locked in. The screams grew into roars at the sound of doors opening and closing. The heavy thunks grew closer as the screams did, the sound of trays being slammed onto the cement becoming clear.

It was the same ritual every morning. The screams and sounds were so familiar that I didn't even move anymore. I just lay on the floor, wishing I hadn't broken the hospital bed last week, and focused on the comfort of the cold cement as the doors continued to slam. Closer and closer.

Arching my body toward the door I waited for mine to open, my heart swelling in need for the brief moment of contact I was about to receive.

Whimpers of joy from the child who was restrained next door replaced his screams before my own door was thrown wide, the only friendly face that existed in this dark place coming into view.

Kaye took one step in and slammed the tray onto the floor,

the action sending brown peas rolling. I didn't even look at the tray anymore, I looked right at her, at her brown eyes, at the way she nodded. I returned the nod, her hand swiping over the ridge of the door frame as she grabbed the note I had left for her. I watched her leave, the low messy bun she now had to wear the last thing I saw before the door slammed between us, closing us off from each other, and me from the one good thing that existed here.

I didn't move.

I lay still, my body pained from sleeping on the cold hard floor, and stared at the food, at the tray, and the little piece of paper that I could see tucked between the divots on the underside. The formed plastic tray was cracked and missing chunks around the edge, which made it the perfect vehicle for note transport.

Trying to focus past the wall of narcotics that Nastya had decided to try on me last night, I reached my unrestrained arm toward the tray. My fingers fumbled against the edge as I desperately tried to grab it. It was just far enough away that I couldn't reach it. I already knew they hadn't given me enough line from my IV to shift closer.

I sighed and rolled over, listening as the sobs of the little boy next door picked back up, the kid calling for his mother as he had since the first day I had been put here. Somehow, the sounds of his cries had become comforting, familiar. I was sure he felt the same way. The way he called for her, the way he spoke to her from time to time.

Sighing, I lifted my arm, the heavy thing wrapped in layers of gauze and bound with a locked brace to keep me away from the IV. The filthy tube trailed from my hand, winding over the floor and through the air until it reached the machines and bags and everything else they used to control and monitor me.

Too high to reach.

Too risky to try.

"A little length next time, would be good," I said, turning toward the camera in the opposite corner, the thing there to make sure I didn't mess up their systems. They couldn't take the risk of giving me full use of my mind and magic after all.

At least they still thought it was working. Shifting my weight, I turned toward the tray, but only the fractured edge hit my fingertips.

Fine. I would have to call this practice.

I pushed myself a little farther toward the tray, letting my magic swell as the tray shifted, the tiny surge of energy bringing the try right to me. Perfect.

I waited for an alarm, or footsteps, or a rush of cold in my IV but nothing happened. They either weren't watching me, or the motion was subtle enough they had missed it.

Didn't matter to me. I had my food, and more importantly, the letter.

Keeping my back to the camera, I huddled over the tray as I poked at the old meat, stomach turning at the once green peas and equally as discolored carrots.

Luckily, I didn't get as sick as many of the others in this prison, but thanks to the IV, I also didn't need to eat as much.

The smell of the meat didn't twist my stomach as much, so I elected to devour that, taking slow bites as I pulled the letter out from underneath the tray.

Countries have fallen. Kyō are coming. Now or never.

I had heard The Kyō mentioned once by Kaye, years before everything changed. Even without hearing more I could already tell that this ominous group could easily be more powerful than the SSU.

"What?" I whispered in Czech as if the single syllable would be magically answered at my demand. There was nothing else.

Nothing more.

I placed the meat in my mouth and immediately spat it out, the taste a million times worse than I expected.

I couldn't eat that, I shouldn't eat that. And yet....

Looking from the note to the unrecognizable slab of meat, I knew there was no choice. I could feel that in the way my heart was thundering in hope. If they were falling, if it was finally happening, I needed strength.

Forcing down the grey square, I pulled my mind from the sludge I was eating and instead attempted to bring my magic up to the surface, using all my strength to break past the barricade of medicated drudgery I was fighting.

With each chew I changed the color of the paper, with each bite I focused my mind and folded it into a new shape, with each swallow I let it hover above the ground, shifting and swimming as it danced. The paper danced and moved, swirling through the air as I swallowed the last bite, the stale meat sitting uncomfortably in my gut.

As the paper fell to the floor, I pushed it to flatten, watching the creases in the paper disappear as those same words winked up at me.

Now or Never.

I had planned to tell her of a memory from the day before, of the tiny village near that house I always dreamed of. Perhaps another clue, yes, but it did not lead to freedom like this would. That news was no longer important.

My heart thundered as I stared at the words, my slow mind struggling to find a way to phrase the questions that buzzed through me in a way that anyone who would find the paper may not understand.

'When do we escape?' was not going to cut it.

Sighing, I popped one of the carrots in my mouth without thinking, the sour rancid flavor turning my stomach. I was barely keeping the meat down, this was not going to help. Spitting the formerly orange blob across the room toward the filthy toilet I pushed the tray away, finally realizing how I needed to phrase it.

Placing my fingertip on the paper, I pushed my magic into it, the power twisting and moving the ink into different shapes.

When can we visit her?

It was enough, and I knew she would get it. I smiled in anticipation, the idea of being able to hold Joclyn seeming impossible after everything. The dream for the future mixed with the dreams of each night and the few precious memories I had and I sighed. Folding the paper back up, I prepared to send it across the floor and into the door frame.

The paper never made it. It fell to the floor as a rush of cold moved through my veins, the faint blue fluid filling the clear IV tube and flooding me like a wave of ice.

I stiffened at the sensation, unable to move as I stared at the paper, the incriminating thing out in the open, my magic frozen enough I couldn't even nudge it.

The cold grew and I knew the paper was not the worst of my problems.

They never took me to her this early.

Something was happening.

A full thought couldn't even break past the numbness that was overtaking me. The world was becoming nothing as I fell forward into what was left of my food, slumping into carrots and peas and some sauce that I had purposefully ignored. I tried to move away from it, but I couldn't move.

The floor began to vibrate as I lay there, the sounds of boots pounding against my skull a second before the doors swung open and the screams began. The heavy metal thing slammed against the supporting wall as at least ten soldiers rushed in, flanked by someone I hadn't seen anywhere other than behind glass for the last few months.

Commander Domor.

I tried to speak his name, but I only gurgled and drooled against the floor. They really had drugged me this time. The disgust on the man's face made his disdain for me clear.

"Take the machine with him," he commanded the soldiers, pointing to the box I was attached to. "Get him in the truck. Your leader is waiting."

The soldiers burst into action as the man sniffed, covering his nose with a handkerchief in an attempt to block the foul smell.

The image made me laugh, he created this, the least he could do is smell it.

Commander Domor stepped outside the room as the soldiers lifted me from the floor, two of them dragging me by the arms as the others flanked our sides with their massive guns drawn and ready.

The other prisoners' screams silenced at seeing the weapons aimed at them, but only because it wasn't normal.

Nothing about this was normal. Instead of going left as I always did, the soldiers dragged me to the right, back through the double doors that led to the cleaner part of the hospital.

The tops of my feet scraped against the floor as they dragged me, the desperate people reaching toward us, grabbing at clothes and feet as if I could help them.

"Get back filth!" the soldiers demanded, bullets flying as they fired above their heads, threatening them to get back, not caring if they hit them, or killed them.

Screams followed the gunfire and the soldiers began to run, my feet sliding over the slick floor, carpet, and then cement before I saw sunlight, true sunlight for the first time in who knew how many years.

Although the light from my dreams had been filled with this same warmth, it hadn't seeped into me like this did. It hadn't infected me. It hadn't been real. This was real, and it was glorious.

I attempted to turn toward the sun, to feel it on my face for the first time, but my head flopped to the side thanks to whatever they had pumped me with. It might as well have been the sun I saw, however.

Kaye was right there.

Kaye, her mother, and a few other nurses I didn't recognize filled one of the military vehicles that sat before the hospital building. Medical equipment, guns, and the electronic machine they had used to torture me for so long were all loaded into the back of another truck, and I was loaded into the back of a third.

The soldiers threw me into the covered bed, arms and legs tangling as I went end over end into a hard metal corner. The perfectly timed steps of the soldiers faded as they marched away, leaving only Commander Domor and me as he jumped into the darkened back of the truck, pulling a pair of metal handcuffs from his pocket.

"Just in case all of that lovely medicine wears off before we get to our new home, eh?" He sneered as he locked my free wrist into the cuff, attaching me to one of the many large rings that lined the bed of the vehicle. "We wouldn't want to lose our most valuable weapon now, would we?"

He laughed again as he clicked the cuff tighter, the metal ring pressing uncomfortably against my emaciated wrist.

My fingers began to tingle at the pressure of the cuff before he ever left the truck, the bed rocking as he jumped through the fabric opening. The flap shifted as he left, letting in one strip of beautiful sunlight before I was left in the dark again. Unable to move, I heaved in air, desperate to calm the panic that was rising in me. The emotion grew as the silence was broken by the sound of gunfire in the distance, the sounds of screams not far behind. Bursts of gunfire accelerated before a massive explosion rocked the ground, truck and limbs shaking at the impact.

The screams swelled, footsteps following as the sound of the bombing continued.

"You can't take it! It's not going to work!" a voice yelled in heavy Ukrainian as the engine of the truck roared to life, sending everything rattling.

"We need him. Nothing works without him."

Kaye.

She was close, right outside the truck, just inches from me.

I needed to get to her. I fought through the drugs, through the fog, and tried to yell, to scream, anything to get her attention. Nothing happened, not even a grunt. I just lay hopelessly against the metal ridges of the truck bed, staring at the cloth of the opening as it flapped in the wind, revealing moments of the chaos outside.

"Meet me at the UK Embassy in Germany," her voice was even closer.

"But it's fallen, too!"

"Then get close!" she screamed. "We don't have time!"

My heart sped up at her proximity, my pulse quickening further as I tried to yell, only to have any effort blocked as another bomb fell, this one right beside us. I attempted to move, to scuttle away and escape the truck, or the war, or whatever it was that was coming. I didn't move an inch, no matter how much work I put into it. I was trapped in the hell the drugs had brought.

The truck roared to life as the earth continued to shake and we began to move, several people beginning to jump in the back with me.

"No, no!" one of the soldiers screamed, the first two who had jumped in obviously sent to guard me. "This is a private transport!"

From where I lay tangled on the floor, I could only see their feet. The two soldiers' boots stood strong before a few others rushed in, three muffled shots sounding loud as the soldiers dropped to the ground, blood pouring from their vacant faces.

"Get in," I heard Kaye shout before someone walked right past me, slamming their fist into the heavy metal that separated truck and cab in a rhythmic four pulse beat. "Let's move!"

She yelled just as the truck took off, roaring to life and speeding away as more guns and more bombs began to rattle the world.

The bombs continued on either side of us as the truck sped along. Each bomb burst through me, a heavy flood of anxiety jerking muscles and heart until the soft touch of fingers against mine took it all away. Kaye's fingers wound through mine as she leaned down, coming into focus in the dark.

"We really must stop meeting like this," she teased, giving my hands a squeeze before they left, moving to cut the large cuff that kept the IV hidden off my arm.

As she worked, the cold in my veins began to fade, the grogginess no longer growing as it had been. My mind began to move, the subtle current of my magic moving back into my fingers. I sighed at the release, attempting to convey my thanks as my tired body settled into the ridged floor of the truck bed. Thankfully, Kaye patted my arm in understanding, moving back to cut the lock that kept the brace against my arm.

"I tried to flush your system earlier, but I didn't expect them to drug you so heavily. I am not sure how long it will take for everything to come back," she said, her focus still on the massive brace on my arm. "Do you feel anything yet?"

I could only moan in response.

"Good," she whispered, carefully moving my head into a position that was thankfully more comfortable. "Just rest, it will get better."

"Who is that?" someone asked in Ukrainian, the voice gruff as we hit a large pothole, the jerk of the vehicle sending everyone jumping.

"Our ticket out of here," she whispered as she began to remove the IV, her motions rough.

"That's him?" the same man asked, his severe face flashing into view as another bomb hit, the truck filling with light as it rocked. "He is the one you have been going on about for months?"

"They have drugged him, Andriey!" Kaye snapped, her face looking even angrier from where I lay below her. "If I can get the drugs out of his system then we might have a chance."

"A chance to what?" Another question, this time from a woman, the faceless voice hissing through the dark. "The man cannot even sit on his own."

"Do you wish to abandon this plan?" Kaye hissed, another bomb swallowing her words as everyone shook and shrieked. "We will not get another chance to escape. And the Kyō... we do not know what will await us."

"Yet you will trust Nastya's puppet," the man again, his voice growing louder as he shifted toward me. "This man cannot even speak."

"I am not a puppet. I was a king." I attempted to sound as powerful as I knew I could be, but the words only came out slurred and mussed.

I wasn't sure if the lack of pronunciation was from the drugs or from spending years in a torture chamber, however. I preferred to think it was the former.

Either way, the response caused the man to jerk, and

although I still could not push myself up to look him in the eye, I turned the best I could, staring him down.

"They drugged me and chained me in the back of the truck." I hissed, the clarity of my words slowly returning. "They do not do that to puppets."

The man glowered at me before leaning back, his eyes still spelling danger. I looked from him to the others, each one either matching my determined scowl with their own, or looking away awkwardly.

There were about ten of them crammed into the small space, and all of them were looking between Kaye and me. The two in the corner were whispering something as they did so.

"Who are these people?" I was suddenly realizing that with all the time Kaye and I had passed notes, I didn't know that much about what she had been doing.

"Workers from the hospital, some of the villagers from nearby." She spoke offhandedly as she peeked out of the jeep again. "They have been working with me. Working against the SSU."

The look she fixed me with was more determined than I had seen, the fight in her finally coming into its own now.

"Are you a rebel leader now?" I asked, the phrase fitting the powerful woman.

She chuckled at the question, but she was the only one, everyone else smiled in response, their respect for her coloring their faces.

"What did you think I meant when I said I was fighting back?" she teased, but I could already tell the others did not agree with that sentiment. "There's a lot I haven't been able to tell you. But once we are free of them, I will."

The admission made me smile. She was right, she had told me, and it suited her.

"What do you need me to do?" My voice was becoming

clearer as I was, the spinning fading as the sound of bombs and guns did.

"As much as you can," Kaye said, loading a few guns as she peeked out of the fabric that covered the truck. "And don't give me lip. I know what you can do, Jan."

"That's not my name," I taunted, slowly pushing myself to sit.

My arms shook under the effort, my brutalized and weakened body struggling to operate. It didn't matter, I had lived with this fog for years, I would push past it. I was powerful, and not just in my dreams.

"Well, let me know when you figure it out," Kaye whispered, helping me to sit up and lean against the truck.

The truck rattled and shook from the uneven road as Kaye handed me a water bottle, the rickety movements sending cold droplets splashing over the dirty cotton bottoms I wore. I grabbed the water greedily, splashing it over my chin as I drank.

"I don't know how much I can do," I said between gulps, desperate for air and water as I slowly felt myself return to normal, even though I knew it would be days before whatever they had been giving me worked its way out completely. "I don't know..."

"You have more control now than you did when you saved me from the Chrlič," Kaye chastised, interrupting me with one look. "You probably have more control even with the drugs."

She looked at me intently, nodding to my hands before fixing me with a glare that only made the magic inside of me buzz more, ready to show her.

Returning the glare, I sagged against the truck, lifting my hands as the magic pulsed deeper, the strength of the surges becoming frightening.

As the drugs began to fade, as my magic began to fight, it was no longer the sludge that I had grown used to, it was the live wire I had only felt in my memories.

Looking from her to my hands, I swallowed, my throat unbelievably dry given the amount of water I had just consumed. The magic roared and rocked just under my skin, surprisingly staying restrained. I had felt less and caused an explosion before. Now, it remained locked in place, until with one thought I sent sparks flying. Electric sparks of the brightest gold jumped between my fingertips, the eruption sending the others in the truck into a panic.

"You trapped us with one of them?"

"He's going to explode!"

They yelled in Ukrainian as they began to scuttle and move, but I couldn't look away from my hands, I couldn't look away from the magic I was now controlling, my command of it focused down to the minutest detail.

"Calm," Kaye snapped, her voice obviously not directed at me. "You must stay calm."

The light grew brighter as I willed it to, the light molding and shifting into a smooth bubble that floated just above my hand, making everything glow.

The truck rattled as another bomb dropped, the entire bed shifting abruptly to the side. We could clearly hear the driver shout something in Ukrainian, his panic filtering through the wall. In the bed of the truck, however, there was only calm.

Everyone stared at the light as I lifted it higher, letting it hover to the top of the canvas. It grew brighter as another bomb dropped, the light exploding in a thousand multicolored lights.

A soft scream echoed over the tent, before a sprinkling of laughter followed, the man who had been so gruff and angry before commenting about how beautiful it was.

"It is," I said, watching the color as another memory tried to move to the surface, something about the way the lights danced seemed familiar.

My hands flew to my lips as the lights fell. The awe turned to screams as the sound of a bomb shook everything and the vehicle soared through the air, the massive machine turning end over end as everything became a tangle of limbs.

I heard the impact before I felt it. Before the hard ridge of the truck bed dug into me, before my mouth filled with dirt and blood. Arms and legs tangled as my screams joined the others, my already pained body rippling with further agony.

It didn't last, however. The magic that was once sludge soared through me, following the aches and breaks and swelling around them, swelling inside of them. Healing me.

I clearly felt a bone snap as the truck came to a stop, a few of us rolling out and over the rubble of what I was sure used to be a city.

Large sections of cement buildings were scattered everywhere. Broken furniture, bloodied clothing, and the haunted face of a child's toy were littered over the ground. I looked right into the green eyes of the doll as my magic throbbed, my jaw clamped as the pain lessened.

"Jan!" I heard Kaye yell from somewhere behind me, but I didn't turn, I wasn't sure I could quite yet. Although the pain was little more than a dull roar now, I didn't trust it enough. I could barely move before the accident, trying now that I had been thrown from a truck seemed like I could be asking too much.

"Jan," she said again, her voice was closer now, the sound of rock and stone shifting just behind me as she stumbled over to my side, her hands rough as she began to turn me over.

"Are you alright?" I asked as she came into focus, my body flopping to the side as she moved me.

"I was going to ask the same of you," she said, each word a

struggle, although the corner of her mouth pulled up a bit. "I've been worse. I have also been better."

The smile didn't hit her eyes and my heart dropped, a fear moving to my toes as I reached for her, glad when she took my hand.

"Don't be scared," I whispered, the words sounding ridiculous when the quick tap of gunfire began in the distance.

Kaye looked at me curiously as I clenched her hand tightly, holding it in a vice grip as I let my magic swell in my hand before pushing it through me and into her.

The magic was different from the accidental healing from all those years ago. It was a flood of heat, and her eyes widened at the sensation, gasping as she tried to shift herself away from me.

"Does it hurt?" I asked in alarm.

"No," she clarified, her eyes wide as she stared at me and my hand. "It's just... warm."

"Good, let me know if it becomes too much."

I let more of it move into her, although I wasn't sure how much was needed, I wanted to be careful. I had never controlled this, after all, I didn't know what was required.

Closing my eyes, I focused the same as I had done in the dream, glad when the magic began to move through her, relaying what felt like whispers of information back to me. Tiny cuts, abrasions, a fractured rib, a bone in her ankle seemed to be out of place. I saw each of them, I felt each of them. My magic pooled around them as she sat before me, her eyes growing wider as one after another they healed, even the cut on the skin above where I held her hand began to knit itself back together.

"Jan," she gasped, eyes wide in shock.

With a sigh, I released her, falling back against the rubble, the world filled with gunfire as those who had been in the back of the truck slowly made their way over to us.

I watched them move, blood pouring from head wounds,

broken bones cradled against them as a few of them limped. I swallowed. I wasn't sure I could heal them all, I was honestly amazed I had been able to control it enough to heal Kaye. Besides, I was sure their reaction to whatever had happened would not be as calm as the powerful woman before me.

"I've never seen it heal that fast," she sighed, still looking at the dried blood that had poured over her arm from where a cut had previously been.

I looked from her to the others in her team, the closest man now within earshot. Only the rumblings of their quick Ukrainian was audible as I lay among rock and steel, listening to the gunfire as it moved closer. It sounded like it was just on the other side of the pile of rubble we had sequestered ourselves against. Their conversation stopped at the sound, Kaye rushing past me until she reached the gentle rise of what was once a building, army crawling over the last of the rubble to look at what was coming.

"There are a few rebels there," she hissed to me and the few others who had joined us, "but they may not hold the line for long.

"Who are they fighting?" one of the older men asked with a groan. The sound of his voice and blood covered arm made it clear he was in pain.

"The SSU. Although I know we passed a depot for The Kyō not far back," Kaye responded as she checked the weapons I had seen her loading before, throwing one to the side when she determined the barrel was no longer safe.

"Trapped between the SSU and the republic," a woman said as she too began to check her weapons, her voice gruff and angry. "Igor picked a hell of a spot to dump us out."

"Where is he, anyway?" the pained man asked over the gunfire, looking from Kaye to the wreckage of the truck that lay about twenty feet behind us. It was only then that I realized how far I had been thrown. No wonder my body was all beat up. It was amazing that I only broke one bone.

"He didn't make it." Kaye didn't look at anyone. "Andriey didn't either. I can't find Yana."

The man swore loudly and spit on the ground while the woman crossed herself and mumbled an old familiar prayer. The other six that stood with us did the same, the same prayer roaring over me and blending with the gunfire in a twisted worship that made my spine twist.

"So we are surrounded," the man said, his voice still hard from his outburst. "By both the SSU and those republic zealots."

I looked to Kaye in question but she only shook her head, there was only one thing I needed to know, and the man had already made that clear.

"How far are we from the border?" he asked as the others finally emerged from their prayer.

Kaye pulled out the same rectangular phone I had seen so many times before, tapping the screen as she brought it to life. The once pristine thing was now dented in several places, the bright screen cracked and flickering. She held it close to her face in an attempt to see and carefully begin hitting the screen. She moved quickly, the screen continuing to flicker before it went out altogether. Two quick taps and it flared back to life, a small sigh escaping her lips.

"It's two miles that way," she sighed, pointing in the direction of the fighting. "If we can make it through that, we can make it out."

Everyone began to nod, the same determination coloring each of their faces. I was sure they had set out from the hospital ready to fight. No escape would be without damage or battle, but their eyes made it clear they hadn't expected this.

They had already fought. Now, it was just survival. It was just two miles to freedom.

I would make sure they made it.

"Now," Kaye said, cocking her small firearm, "who can walk?"

I wanted to say that the question was for everyone, but she was looking right at me.

"I can do more than walk," I said, shifting myself to sitting as my body ached from so many years of ill use. None of that mattered now.

"I think I can fly."

12

JOCLYN

WE LAY flat on our backs on top of one of the tall buildings that surrounded the hospital. We were doing our best not to be seen, even though we had both realized it was pointless at this point.

"I don't know if I should complain we are here too late, or be excited for the battle," Ryland moaned from where he lay beside me, thankfully not looking as green as he had a few minutes ago.

"This is definitely going to make finding them a bit harder." My stomach was already in knots and this was making it worse.

We had, somewhat foolishly, assumed that we would get here before the Kyō army would. The Kyō, however, had clearly already been heading this way when news of them 'taking control' of every country had spread.

"Harder? Or easier?" Ryland said, that eager grin he always got before battle making a return. Sometimes he looked so much like his brother it made my heart cleave in two.

But not this time, not with Ilyan so close.

"What do you mean?" I asked, twisting to the side as I looked at him.

"Well, look at it," Ryland said, making a sweeping motion

toward the hospital. "The place is in shambles. Chances of anyone noticing us when we walk in are slim to none now."

He had a point. When I had seen the hospital in my sight it had been calm, in fact it almost looked abandoned. But now, soldiers were everywhere. They were breaking windows as they threw equipment out of them so they could load the trucks. They were trying to build lines around the hospital to stop the Kyō armies as they got closer, fashioning whatever equipment they didn't want to pack into some of the shabbiest barricades I had ever seen.

The army Ryland and I had seen the other day was nowhere to be found. These soldiers didn't have magic, but the Kyō did.

Just laying here, I could hear the fighting growing closer, the SSU armies that had been sent through the streets after the Kyō were growing closer.

Essentially, we only had until those armies got here to find him. We were looking at a ticking time bomb.

"So, you are suggesting we just walk in and find him?" I asked as a line of trucks pulled up to the front of the hospital. I scanned the backs and fronts, looking for the woman from the tent, the woman I had seen torture Ilyan. Except for the very scattered looking drivers these trucks were empty.

"Yep. You'll be able to sense Ilyan's magic, probably even Míra's. Chances are, knowing Míra, she has already found him and is running through that mess like she's on a spy mission." I couldn't help but smile at that, I knew he was right.

That was, assuming that they were both okay. Reason number one for why we needed to get in there.

"Okay, let's go." I stood, dusting off the knees of my jeans as I prepared to hurl myself into the building and find my mate.

I could already feel my magic boiling right to the surface, pulling through the air as it searched him out. I could feel it pull me into the chaotic halls; as though it had already found its other half.

I pulled Ryland up, ready to go when the phone in my pocket began to buzz.

I told Thom and Wyn not to contact me unless it was an emergency, and here they were -- contacting me. I glared at my phone even before I pulled it out, already knowing I wasn't going to leave for anything. Even a coup.

I wasn't going to leave Ilyan behind, we were too close.

The screen flared to life, Ryland looking over my shoulder as the text loaded.

'Her name is Nastya Klotz. She's the head of the SSU and has been torturing Ilyan for years. She wants you. Be careful. It's a trap.'

I was instantly raging. All of my magic boiling right to the tips of my fingers as the word torture played on repeat. Each time it beat through my head it got louder until it was all I could hear. I didn't know how Thom and Wyn had gotten this information, and I didn't care. It was all I needed to go in and rip that entire place to shreds.

Ryland laughed beside me, the humorless sound ripping me out of the murderous rage that was quickly growing in my head.

"Did Thom really think that we should be worried about walking into a trap after telling you that this woman has been torturing your husband for years?" He laughed again, but I was staring at the hospital, almost desperate to find the woman now.

I barely saw Ryland turn out of the corner of my eye. His laugh stopped short as he saw me, standing there, staring at the hospital with laser eyes.

"Or he knew exactly what he was doing," Ryland mumbled, his hand warm on my shoulder as he pulled my focus. "You ready Jos? Not like I really have to ask."

"Let's find this bitch." I took off without even waiting for him.

My magic gathered, circling around me in a powerful wave

that took me right into the air, over the lot that was filled with trucks and right onto the roof of the hospital.

If Ilyan was here, I was going to find him, and together we would make that woman pay for what she had done.

Ryland landed right behind me, already running toward the buzzing energy that I was sure he felt just as strongly as I did. Magic, poisoned magic, just a little bit ahead, maybe two feet down. Ryland had gone on so many tracking missions over the past three years that I let him pull ahead, his magic already surging as he held his hand out and sent one blast into the roof.

A stream of black slammed into the cement and asphalt, shaking the hospital as though it had been hit by a bomb.

Because it had.

Ryland's attack hadn't been the only one. The Kyō had apparently arrived, and were blasting their way in just as we were.

"Well, this just got dangerous," Ryland said, turning back as he pulled to a stop before the now gaping hole in the roof. "The race is on. Who will find Ilyan first."

I didn't like that. Just thinking about it made my stomach twist and writhe. We should have left last night. We had waited, and now everything was shifting.

Keeping Thom's text message in mind, I jumped into the hole, landing on cracked linoleum as I searched for any sign of the magic users we felt, or of that woman.

The hallway was empty. There was nothing but cracked walls, blinking lights, and forgotten medical supplies.

Creepy as hell. "No one is here."

"Going down," Ryland announced as he landed beside me, already blasting a hole into the floor and taking us down closer to the pulsing veins of broken magic we had sensed on the roof.

Now it was fading, almost as though the owners were being led away.

"Hurry," I spat, mostly to myself as I jumped through yet another hole and fell into hell. "What in the world?"

This was not the run down hospital hallway of a floor up. This was cement walls and stained floors. This was bare lightbulbs swinging from wires and the smell of human excrement. This was where you put the people you hated most.

I ran to the first open door, to a child's drawings that were painted on the floor with things I didn't want to think about. I bolted across the hall to another, to chains so coated in blood they looked red, and then to a third, to a plastic lunch tray with untouched food and a slip of paper on the ground.

I picked it up, the edges torn and paper worn as though it had been folded and unfolded hundreds of times. It only had four words on it, the handwriting close to chicken scratches: *When can we visit her?*

I showed the slip of paper to Ryland, but he was just as lost as I was. Nothing about this place made sense.

"Do I really want to know what was going on in here?" Ryland asked behind me as I walked further into the room, grabbing the IV off the ground. The long tube went to a box in the corner, whatever all of these people had been pumped with still dripping through in slow drops of the brightest blue.

It didn't look normal.

"Is it anything like what you saw at the Kyō?" I asked, dropping the IV as I raced out of the room and back into the hall.

"Maybe. They were all connected to tubes, but without seeing who was here, it's hard to know."

I nodded. I hadn't seen the monstrosities the Kyō had created, and my mind was already running away with what we had just seen. People were kept here. Ilyan might have been kept here...

All of the rage that had rampaged through me since I had read the text message turned into a firestorm.

God. I was going to kill someone before all of this was over.

"Let's find them shall we?" My face twisted up into a mutated smile as I shoved my magic away from me. I let it pour through the air, smothering every hall filled with terrified soldiers, into every line of nurses as they tried to make their escape.

I poured every bit of my magic into those halls as I looked for him. He was close. He had to be. But nothing.

No trace of him.

I did, however, find the same magic we had felt before, the twisted brokenness of unhealed magic was like a beacon.

"This way." I grabbed Ryland's sleeve and pulled him after me, both of us racing down the hall as a crash echoed through the building.

The sound of glass and stone shattering filled the halls as everything under us shifted.

"Seems the Kyō are taking it up a step," Ryland mumbled as we raced, both of us turning a corner as the feeling of that broken magic came closer.

"Almost there," I said more to myself than anyone, just as another bomb exploded somewhere to the left, sending the whole building rocking as it nearly collapsed. I only barely caught myself with my magic, lifting us up as the floor beneath us fell away.

"Going down," I said as I flew through the hole, rushing toward what I could clearly make out as the massive tile and glass entrance hall to the hospital.

"You know, if we make it out of here alive," Ryland said as he caught up with me, the hospital creaking as yet another explosion rattled from somewhere deep within, "I call dibs on the leader of the Kyō. I think I've about had it with him."

"He's all yours. But Nastya Klotz is mine." I turned to him, giving him a grin as we raced toward the door and the buzzing feeling of magic. Except he had stopped.

Ryland stood in the middle of the giant entry hall, the last of the soldiers running out as the building threatened to come down.

"Ryland, come on!" I rushed back to him, grabbing his hand. I was fully ready to pull him out of here if I needed to. "Ry!"

He turned to me slowly, his eyes wide. If it wasn't for all the dust in the air I would have sworn he was crying.

"She's down there."

"Who?" I yelled, still pulling on his hand.

"Míra."

He didn't need to say any more. We were already running.

13

MÍRA

"THE REPORTS ARE COMING in from many different sources, all of which talking about how the might of the SSU will reign victorious through this challenge..."

"Reign victorious," I scoffed, undoing the last of my straps as I glanced at the fogged glass on either side of the door again. "I'm pretty sure none of you all really think you are going to reign victorious."

It was absolute chaos out there.

It hadn't been the TV that had woken me up, it had been the armies preparing for war inside the hospital. It had been the gunshots that rattled through the halls.

The news shows that were playing on my television night and day were nothing more than propaganda, but anyone with half a brain and one eye could figure it out.

Less than two days ago the Kyō had taken over every country save a few, the ones where the SSU were if I had to venture a guess.

And, based on the absolute panic that was outside my room, the Kyō had come to claim the final prize.

My time here was up. It was time I found Ilyan and got us out of here.

And I had been so looking forward to conducting all the espionage. Good thing there was still the Kyō to deal with. I just hoped that Joclyn didn't go all crazy and take them out in her search for me.

Seeing as they were the last ones I was technically with I wouldn't be surprised if she went there first. How were they to know Michel was essentially bowing to everyone *but* Joclyn. He sold me to the highest bidder.

Who happened to be Nastya.

"Don't forget, you promised her you would cut her head off," I reminded myself as I jumped off the bed, padding toward the door where shouts of panic had begun to echo through the halls.

I opened the door, the hinges squeaking as loudly as they always had. Not that anyone noticed.

The hallway was in pure chaos. Even my guards were gone. I bet I could walk through the hall in my backless hospital gown and no one would notice.

Why not? I was always up for a challenge.

I cracked my knuckles and neck like those kung fu fighters you see in movies and stepped into the war zone.

"Everyone to the east side!"

"No, to the west!"

The confusing commands in Ukrainian echoed from everywhere, the soldiers rushing around in a confusing pattern. I weaved under two men with large guns, around a crying nurse, and hid behind a bed as I slowly made my way to the same nurses' station that I had tried to Stutter into before.

The only lead I really had for finding Ilyan in this place was Katenka and her younger clone. I might as well head to the last place I saw them and hope for the best.

"Search to the left! I need eyes." A shout came from the end of the hall, near my room. Those soldiers were always a step behind me. Poor souls.

I ducked behind the counter at the nurses' station as five guards stormed past, another two running in the other direction.

"They need help in the blood wing!"

Ooo Blood Wing. That sounds cool.

Looks like we have a winner.

The soldier that had shouted it was already heading in the other direction, running through the crowd in a panic. I snapped a shield into place, important now that people were looking for me, and darted behind him, doing my best to follow. I was dodging soldiers the best I could, well aware that while they may not even notice if I ran into them, it wasn't worth the risk. I would just fly above their heads and be done with it, but I was pretty sure that a phantom wind through a hospital hallway was not going to go unnoticed.

I darted down a hall that was clogged with soldiers, patients lined up against the hall as they screamed and pulled at the soldiers for help. I needed to avoid that.

I turned in the other direction when one of the soldiers fired gunshots into the air and everyone swarmed in the exact direction I was heading. Unable to see me, I was pushed down, swept to the side and nearly trampled to death.

Okay, running around invisible wasn't working. The halls were a wave of black uniforms and yellow sunbursts, guns clacking against armor and pointing as everyone raced. I had already lost track of the guy headed to the blood wing.

"This is bullshit," I said as I tried to dodge around one guy, only to have another smack me in the back of the head with the butt of his gun.

Even if I was being searched for, people would at least

naturally avoid me if they could see me. Besides, I could take them if they found me.

I shifted my shield around, pulling myself back into view and continuing my race after the guy who was heading to the blood wing. I moved like some kind of super spy, darting around soldiers and medical equipment until I froze at the messy brown bun that was racing out the door.

Katenka.

Exactly who I was looking for. She turned when she reached the front door, her thin face coming into view. Not Katenka, the daughter. This was even better.

I stretched my magic out as I followed her, trying to sense the strength of her power, but found nothing. I hadn't been wrong had I? I mean, the girl had legit disappeared before. She had to have magic.

Guess it would just be the first thing I asked when I found her.

I quickly changed direction, continuing my darting and weaving as I tried not to lose her. She was good at this, no wonder she had disappeared before.

Katenka's daughter raced right out the front doors and to a row of trucks that were being loaded with all of the machinery I had seen in Nastya's torture chamber.

That and guns. So many of those long black guns that all the soldiers carried. I guess I was in the right place after all.

I hugged the wall of the building, edging myself closer to where mini-Katenka was talking with at least ten others who were huddled around the back of a car about fifty yards away.

"Are you sure this is going to work, Kaye?" one of them asked, thankfully giving me her name, although mini-Katenka was growing on me.

"Trust me, I'm sure," Kaye said, grabbing one of the guns out of the back of the car as she began to change out of her nurse's uniform and into a soldier's.

Ooo perfect. Clean clothes. I took a step forward, ready to make my introduction, find Ilyan and get home.

"We just have to move quickly or--" Anything she had been about to say, and any saucy introduction I had been about to make, was lost to the whistling sound of a bomb seconds before the buildings on the other side of the parking lot exploded.

"Shit!" I yelled, loud enough that one of the people Kaye had been talking to turned, staring at me in all of my hospital gown glory.

"Let's go!" Kaye screamed, just as another bomb dropped and they all began to race toward the trucks I had seen being loaded.

Everything was chaos now, soldiers were screaming and running back into the hospital. People were throwing things into trucks that were already moving as people raced to escape the bombs that were now dropping in earnest.

Dust choked the air, and in turn my lungs as I struggled to keep up. Kaye and the others were only ten feet ahead of me, my focus so intent on them that I missed the whistling sound from right overhead.

Another bomb exploded just a few feet to my left, rocks flew over me, shoving me to the side and right into the glass wall of the hospital. Glass scraped over marble, stone cracked, I could have sworn the building was creaking. But, that might have just been my magic as it snapped through me, pressing a bone or two back together.

I stood, shaking my head as my vision slowly settled, the world continuing to tremble as bomb after bomb exploded through the building. Wind rushed past me, rocks freckling my skin as I took a step and froze at the woman who was racing back into the building.

Nastya.

Blood pulsed through my ears in an angry throb as I took a step toward her. I froze, glancing out the doors, but the trucks were already gone. Yes, Kaye probably knew where Ilyan was. But so did Nastya.

Besides, I had a promise to keep.

"One head, coming right off," I whispered, smiling as I ran after her.

The hospital rattled around me, the floor shifting as I raced down the hall that was somehow growing colder with each step. The whole building quaked as a bomb exploded somewhere far too close for comfort. The motion sent us both into the side wall, where glass shattered and showered over us like rain.

Stabby rain that cut into my skin.

"You gonna keep running, or are you going to let me finish this right now?" I yelled as she pulled herself to her feet, clearly intending to keep running.

Nastya looked back at me, her lip curling. I guess she hadn't realized I was here. She really didn't have good control of her magic if she hadn't sensed me just feet from her. Then again, her magic was still that drippy broken stuff before Joclyn healed it.

That kind of magic didn't work quite right. I would know, I was trained with it.

"Finish what?" Nastya asked with that coy voice of hers. "You really don't think you could take me on, do you?"

She smiled at me in big headed victory, her magic dripping from her fingertips like sludge in what she clearly thought was a threat.

"God. You are *really* full of yourself." I stepped toward her, double checking that my shield was still in place. Just in case she got lucky. "You're like one of those tiny dogs who doesn't realize they are facing a big dog and just snaps and bites anyway."

"Did you forget our little playtime the other day so easily,"

Nastya asked, magic still pooling from her fingers as she stepped closer.

"You mean when you had me strapped to a table and thought you had restrained my magic? Naw." I shrugged, lifting my hands for the first time and letting my own magic flow. But instead of sad little wet ribbons of magic it crackled between my fingers, swelling and growing into a crackling ball of power. "I didn't forget. I just used it."

I threw the ball then, right into her horrified face. She wasn't so smug now as she practically threw herself into the wall to avoid my attack. Her breath came in sharp little pants as she slipped on glass and rocks in a panic to get away from me.

I just rolled my eyes, some Queen Almighty she was.

My magic pulsed once as I stepped forward, into the Stutter and across the hall right in front of where she was running. She screamed and ducked, hands over her head.

"Really? You aren't even going to try to make this a tad bit interesting?" I wiggled my fingers, preparing to attack, and instead found myself falling sideways into the floor as she swept my foot. Rookie mistake.

She jumped over me, already attacking, but I just Stuttered a bit to the left and attacked her. She dodged, although barely.

"Yes! Let's tango! I'm ready!" I shot another attack at her, and this time she countered, although her magic didn't have enough oomph behind it to truly block me. Half of my attack sped through, slamming into her gut and throwing her back down the hall.

The hospital shook, groaning as another bomb hit it from somewhere above. This building might not last very long.

Okay, time to get back on track.

"Tell me where Ilyan is!" I yelled as I rushed over to her, my hands pointing at her menacingly.

"Who?" she asked, her voice actually shaking.

"Ilyan! I know you have him!" She still looked at me as though I was speaking gibberish. Good lord, could she really not know who she had? "Blond guy. The Oheň's partner."

That did the trick, recognition flared in her eyes, the panic from before fading as she began to laugh.

Okay, that was not what I was expecting.

"Where is he?" I repeated again, even though I was well aware my resolve was slipping. I sent a zap of power into her in warning, just in case.

She just kept smiling. Smiling and laughing like the loon she was.

"He's already gone. I just put him on a truck myself."

I turned, hands still trained on her as I looked back to the bay of trucks that had already left. The ones filled with the machinery. She wasn't lying.

"Seems I should have followed the trucks instead of you," I said, shrugging my shoulders before I turned back to her. "Doesn't matter though. Like I said, I had a promise to keep."

I didn't even wait for her to protest before I cut off her head.

14

ILYAN

KAYE'S EYES WIDENED, the others looking at me as though I had spoken gibberish. I may as well have. I wouldn't have believed it if I hadn't seen it in my dreams. If I hadn't seen myself teach Joclyn to fly.

The admission had my magic erupting. A breeze played around my toes, the memory of throwing Nastya away from me all those years ago replaying softly in the back of my mind.

I couldn't stop the grin.

"But bullets..." Kaye said, her voice a soft reminder of my fear, and perhaps my limitations.

"Maybe I am bulletproof, Kaye," I said, my smile growing as the eager joy spread. "There is no better time to find out."

Kaye's smile rose to join mine, the grin spreading just as wide as she realized what was about to happen.

"We need to get through whatever is on the other side of this rise," her voice was hoarse as she nodded her head toward the gunfire just on the other side of the rise. "If we can get through that then it should be a straight shot to the border."

Magic swelling inside of me, I nodded once before closing my eyes, letting the power swell into the air.

Me following right behind.

The men and women in Kaye's group began to shout in shock, their voices drowned out by the wind as it picked me up, my body wobbling and shaking as I worked to control it.

"Focus only on the wind. Focus on its movement, on its warmth. Focus on how your magic will bring it to you." My own words whispered through memory, the phrasing unknown to me, although I knew at once what it was talking about.

So I obeyed.

My body began to stabilize as I closed my eyes, magic swelling further as more and more of the drugs began to wear off.

Smiling, I hovered before the group, all of them in different states of awe and fear, all except for Kaye. Kaye stood beneath me with the widest smile on her face, the sheer joy out of place as she stood against the rubble.

"Be ready," I said, only waiting for Kaye to nod her head in acknowledgment before I took off, soaring over the remains of the old building and toward the fight below.

About twenty black-clad soldiers marched below me, their chests all stamped with the sinister star that I now abhorred. Cleaners.

The Cleaners were closing in on a small group of disheveled militia that were taking stock of their weapons from behind a rise even smaller than the one Kaye and her people were behind.

The rebels were the ones to see me first, their shock and fear rising as they began to lift their weapons. It was only when Kaye and her men ran over the rise that they calmed, but the quiet was short lived.

The Cleaners turned at the noise, guns pointed toward Kaye before one after another they caught sight of me, hovering above them. Judging by the looks on their faces, even without my hair, they knew exactly who I was.

Guns shaking, they lifted them to the sky, twenty black muzzles pointed right at me.

In a staccato explosion of sound the guns fired, tiny blasts of flame shooting from the muzzles as a dozen bullets cut through the air toward me.

Steeling my courage, I shoved my hands forward, heart pounding as an absolute wave of yellow erupted from my fingers. The wall of magic spread away from me like a net, little sparks of red popping against it as the bullets were devoured. As everything was devoured. Soldiers screamed as they scattered like ants, the one man who couldn't leave fast enough turning to ash as the magic met him.

Shouts of fear and awe echoed around the clearing as both sides saw what happened. Rebels took off running, soldiers scattered to a new formation as they were joined by others, the black-clad army breaking through the trees. The Cleaners formed a wide circle as they surrounded me on all sides, necks craning toward me as their guns rose as one. With a single snap of a command, bullets soared from all directions, hurtling through the air toward me.

This wasn't the one-sided barrage I had been hit with before. I couldn't engulf everything in flames to stop it, the rebels were still there, sneaking through the rubble toward the city, Kaye and a few others picking off the Cleaners one by one.

With a sharp inhale I pressed the power away from me, creating a wave that I hoped would knock out bullets and Cleaners. While I heard screams of pain, saw the faint pops of light as bullets exploded, I couldn't get them all. The bullets kept coming.

Bringing my magic to me, I let it swallow me as I tried in vain to recreate the shield I had felt in memory before. Keeping the moment as I ran through the burning forest with Joclyn clear in my mind, I tried to replicate the magic, replicate the feeling.

I was almost successful.

The clear barrier rippled in light and air as each bullet hit it, sending the now flat disks falling to the ground. All but one. The single bullet ripped through the barrier before it ripped through my flesh, the sound of my magic disintegrating a faint pop before it was drowned by my scream.

The agony was one I had felt so often that the scream was almost wasted, except for the fact that I was now tumbling to the ground, limbs twisting as I desperately attempted to focus my magic through the pain and protect myself from a devastating impact.

Wind surrounded me in a rush, billowing around me as it tried to lift it up, only to have the sensation quickly replaced by that of the rock hard ground slamming against my bones. The agony increased as the pain spread, my own stubbornness rising up as I quickly clamped my lips around the scream, refusing to let it escape.

"Jan!" Kaye's scream ripped through the pulses of gunfire as she rushed to my side, sliding against rubble and dirt in her attempt to reach me faster.

Dirt sprayed over me, but that was hardly my biggest worry.

I reached in vain for the bullet that was now lodged in my back, the foreign object pulsing painfully against me as my body attempted to heal.

"Take it out," I gasped as my awkward fingers slipped over blood and fabric, trying to claw at the skin.

I would rid myself apart to get it out if I had to.

"Layno," Kaye swore, her voice agitated as she rolled me onto her lap. My lungs heaved as I lay over her legs, my ragged breathing increasing as she ripped the back of my shirt open. "I don't have tweezers, Jan. This is going to hurt."

"Just get it out!" I yelled, my voice similar to the commands that I gave so often in my dreams.

Thankfully, she didn't wait.

After one shaky exhale, her fingers pressed against the jagged opening of my skin, preparing for the deep dive.

"This area is clear, Kaye," a voice said, the crunching of rocks and dirt signaling the arrival of one her soldiers, and the end of the Cleaners. "We can mo... what are you doing?"

The voice had gone from calm to panic faster than I could count. Which I couldn't because all my focus was on getting this thing out of my back.

"Removing the bullet," Kaye said matter of factly, a new pain beginning to ripple over me as she ripped and clawed at my flesh.

"What?" The man was aghast, his outrageous fear giving me something to focus on. "Do not do that here! Bind him! He could bleed out."

I pinched my eyes shut as the pain grew, clenching my jaw in defiance as Kaye worked harder, pulling at skin in an attempt to get at the bullet that was lodged inside me.

"No, he won't," Kaye said, her patience was strained as she continued to work, the warmth of my own blood clear as it began to pour down my back.

"But he..."

"Got it," Kaye interrupted the man, the pressure growing for one brief moment before it lessened, my back feeling like it was being suctioned before the weight was gone, fingers and bullet no longer blocking my magic from what it did best.

"What..." The question stopped short with the weird clicking noise the man made as I stood, the last drop of blood rolling down my back as the wound began to close.

"Thank you, Kaye," I whispered, turning toward her with a

nod that right then, with all we had gone through, was not enough.

"I forgot how tall you were," she said with a smile, forcing out a chuckle as she shifted her weight uncomfortably. I couldn't help but laugh at that, the sound rich and loud, and decidedly out of place for the war zone we were in.

Even with the time and growth that had passed, Kaye still only came to my sternum. Just like Joclyn.

Joclyn.

"We have to move," I said, that same commanding tone coming on strong.

I didn't even try to restrain it, and no one questioned it. I was right, after all, we were so close to the border, to freedom.

I was so close to finding her.

"Right," Kaye said, taking her phone out of her pocket as she pointed to a cluster of old buildings right before a tree line to our left. "The border is just beyond those trees there. If we get into the trees we should be free. The Belarusians have been sympathetic to our plight from what I have read."

"Let's hope that holds true," one of the men from the truck said, checking his weapons.

Kaye only nodded.

"I will fly above, as sentry," I added, something about the commands I was giving comforting. "If we head straight through the homes to the left I think we will be okay. There may be fewer places for the enemy to hide." I pointed, many of them following the line as they nodded their heads in agreement. Kaye, however, looked right at me with a look that screamed with an awe so familiar that my soul rebelled against it, the motion twisting and turning in my gut so strongly that it was all I could do not to step away.

"Just stay together," I finished lamely, the words choking awkwardly as I realized where I had seen that look before.

In Joclyn, in my dreams.

No.

That look did not belong on her.

It was then that I did step away.

"Go," I said as her face fell, taking off into the air before she or anyone else could say another word.

The rebels organized far below me, checking guns and ammo as they began their sprint toward the houses, picking up weapons off the soldiers as they moved. I stayed above them, heart clenching tightly as Kaye looked up to me, the concern clear on her face before it was swallowed by walls and buildings.

They moved into the house lined streets in a double line, each side continually monitoring alleys and streets and windows as they moved through them. While the motions were awkward and unpracticed I could see a skill there, the technique wrought in the determination to survive.

Pulling my focus from the group, I let my magic swell, the power keeping me airborne as I prepared for an attack, or a bomb, or anything else that could foil our plan.

I wouldn't let that happen. I needed to get them to safety. Kaye needed her freedom, and I would do anything to give that to her.

Magic pulsed as loud as my heartbeat in my ears. I let out a shaky breath, letting the expulsion swallow the anxiety.

Although the edge of the city and the start of the forest was growing closer, those below were slowing down. Their pace slower, breathing slower.

That couldn't be right.

Not this close.

They should be running.

They were, I realized with a start, they were running. I was the one who was slowing down. I was the one who was falling behind.

My magic waned as a residual wave of the medicine ran through me. Head spinning, I lost a foot of height, magic shifting as I struggled to keep control.

As I struggled to bring it back.

Just as the air broke with gunfire.

Faint pops broke through the fog that surrounded me, one coming right after another as the assault came right at me. My sluggish magic barely kept me in the air, so, with the roared command for the others to run, I propelled myself forward, using the only thing I had to keep me from the gunfire. Momentum.

Without the circle of the attack as before, I was able to flee from it, soaring past it fast enough that not even one of the bullets slammed into me.

My magic stuttered as the wind left and I was jerked through the air again, free falling a few feet before I was able to recover. Thankfully the magic returned at once, lifting me back up to where I was.

It was enough time to breathe.

It was also enough time for them to reload.

One after another the sharp pointed bullets plunged into my body, ripping through flesh and bone as they destroyed me.

There was no stopping it this time. I didn't even have a chance.

The magic was gone as the bullets sunk into me, more digging into flesh and grinding against bone as I fell. This time I hit the ground hard, legs crumpling underneath me as the sound of my bones physically breaking echoed like their own brand of gunfire.

The scream from the rebels broke out as their gunfire did. The two sides shooting at each other as some chose to fight, some chose to run.

I could see Kaye from where I lay, crumpled on the ground, the pool of my own blood staining the dirt around me.

She fired at whoever had hit me in spurts, sending puffs of gunfire back before she would duck behind cars and corners, those in the building doing the same.

It was a masochistic dance of back and forth, each party tiptoeing around each other until one side stopped, and Kaye was left huddled behind a rock. Waiting. Waiting.

She peeked out at me from the side, our eyes meeting each other, before, with a quick staccato beat of gunfire, more than a dozen bullets rained over me.

I didn't even scream.

I wasn't sure I could.

Kaye's soft whimpers bled through the air from where she hid, until she streaked toward me, grabbing underneath my arms and dragging my body into the dark shadows of an alley. Flopping down beside me, her hands fluttered over me, trying to decide which bullet to remove first.

"There are too many," I hissed, my voice a weak groan as I attempted to move before I decided that even that was too much. "You need to get out of here, Kaye."

"You think after all of that I am just going to leave you?" As much as she tried to make her voice strong and powerful, she couldn't disguise it through the tears. The pain was too much. The devastation was too much.

"You have to," I sighed, barely able to muster enough strength to grab her hand. "You promised you would."

"I..." She stopped, glancing up as the sound of doors and footsteps echoed through the alley between houses and right to us.

"Run, Kaye," I hissed, blood filling my mouth.

She hesitated, shifting her weight before she looked down the street, my focus following hers as we looked away from the quickly advancing troops and toward the line of safety just behind.

The trees swayed in a happy little dance, the supposed safety of the other country screaming for us.

For her.

"You have to go," I pleaded, squeezing her hand once before I dropped it. "Run."

I could hear the shouts from the soldiers behind us now, the rough Russian mixing with Mandarin in a way I would have never expected.

"Go. Find Joclyn. Tell her I love her."

"I will find her. I will come back, Jan," she whispered, her body bouncing in hesitation.

"That's not my name," I said sternly, but this time she didn't even smile, she just looked at me sadly, tears rolling down her cheeks.

"I know." She leaned down, pressing her lips firmly against my forehead before she turned and ran.

I rolled over with a shout, letting my magic pour from my outstretched fingers as I tried to protect her, to stop the bullets that were now flying over my head toward her.

She needed to get out of here.

She needed to be free, to be safe.

The wall of color that streamed from my hand slowly began to fade as more bullets plunged into my body, blood pouring from me. My magic tried to fight it, tried to heal me, but there were too many.

It was too much.

15

RYLAND

"Míra!"

I wasn't even sure if she heard me over the rumble of the building, the groan of the wood and steel was deafening as we ran to where Míra stood over Nastya Klotz, the woman's hair in her hands.

"Míra!" I tried again, my heart exploding in my chest with its need to get to her. Joclyn ran beside me, but for everything in the world it might as well have just been me, racing down the hall to save the woman my magic had bonded to.

Even if it was *very* clear that she did not need any saving.

Míra said something to Nastya, shrugging her shoulders as I felt her magic buzz through the air, a streak of white fanning from her palm like a sword. Not a second later she swiped it through the air, right through the neck of Nastya Klotz.

Her body fell away, crinkling like a rag doll's as Míra stood there, holding a severed head by the hair.

"No!" Joclyn yelled, her magic carrying her the rest of the way. Míra looked up, still holding the head as her face broke out into a wide grin.

"Ryland!" Something in my chest snapped at seeing her there, that wide grin on her face, so excited to see me.

I raced to her, gathering her up in my arms. She was so small, so frail. And an absolute powerhouse.

"You found me," she whispered, that vulnerability in her voice that she always saved for me sneaking through.

"I did." I ran my hand down her hair as I held her to me, as she wrapped her arms around me and Nastya's severed head beat against my back. I stiffened. "You know. I think hugging you while you are holding a severed head might go down as the weirdest thing we have ever done."

"Oh! Sorry!" Mira gasped, wiggling out of my grasp. Her smile was still in place. "But believe me when I say she deserved it. Bitch was running electricity through my veins and cutting open my arms and crap. I'm sure she did the same to Ilyan."

"Ilyan." Jos gasped from where she stood over Nastya's body, her eyes filled with tears. For half a second I actually thought she might have been mourning the fallen dictator. "How are we going to find him now?"

Her tears turned to rage in less than a second, and without thinking I stood between Jos and Mira. Even though I wasn't sure exactly who I was protecting. My oath said one, my heart said another. This was getting confusing.

Especially considering that Mira was still holding a head, and still smiling.

"Don't worry, I got some good intel from her before I killed her." Mira held up the head, grinning at her like the lifeless appendage could see her. "I know where he is."

"Then what the hell are we waiting for?" Joclyn screamed, all of her rage and frustration building through her voice as a bomb dropped and the building creaked again.

This place was coming down and Joclyn's magic was moving it along.

"This way!" Míra called, already running back toward the entryway that we had just come from.

"Míra," I panted as I caught up to her. "I'm glad we found you--"

"So am I." She grinned at me, I just continued on.

"And I am going to assume you are perfectly fine."

"I am, even if this bitch tried to break me." She held up the head again.

"But can we ditch the head?" It wasn't really a question. Míra looked at me, and then the head as we turned the corner.

"But I thought I could hang it on--"

"No head, Míra." Joclyn snarled from the other side of her. Míra's face fell at the command, but the knots in my stomach were already loosening. Míra might be the only person I knew who would try to accessorize with a severed head.

"Remind me to station you with someone besides Wyn for a while," Joclyn said as we raced through the broken glass of the front door, the building still screaming of its impending collapse behind us.

Well, and Wyn. Joclyn was probably on to something.

"Fine, fine, but first," Míra pointed toward the outskirts of Kiev and the border Ukraine shared with Belarus beyond. "Nastya told me she loaded everyone in trucks going that way. Ilyan should be with them."

Joclyn exploded into the air, the rush of her magic whipping our hair around as we stood, watching her fly, yet another bomb exploding into the air behind her. She almost looked like a Fourth of July firework.

"Are you okay?" I whispered to Míra, refusing to look away from where Joclyn was arching through the air.

"Awww.... Ryland! Were you worried?" she teased, her hand firm on my arm as she pushed me to the side. Then I looked at her, looked at the sarcastic smile that was doing its best to hide all the hurt she didn't want anyone else to see. Looked at the blood on her hands and the mud on her nose.

"You saved my life, and then you were gone. I worried."

"Well, worry no more. I'm here to help you kick some ass." She put her hands on her hips like some kind of superhero and then took off into the air with one fist in the air. She soared right up to Jos, both of them looking over the landscape as magic began to explode from every angle.

They just looked so cool.

And I was staring way too long.

We may have found Míra, but she was not the only person we had come for.

They darted through the air in the direction of the trucks and all of the muscles in my back pulled into tight coils, my stomach twisting as I took off after them. I had only just caught up to them, all of us racing toward the lines of trucks that were barreling towards the border, when something exploded next to them.

It looked like someone had bottled an electrical storm and turned it into a bomb. The ground exploded, dirt and rocks and pieces of trucks arcing into the air as blast after blast hit around where the trucks had been.

"No!" Joclyn shouted before she disappeared, pulling herself into a Stutter and right to where Ilyan should be.

"Ry!" Míra yelled, holding out her hand, but I avoided contact. Like hell if I was going to risk that again.

"Don't even think about it! You go! Help her! I'll be there." Míra gave me a pug faced pout but didn't fight me before her magic sparked and she vanished, following Joclyn to somewhere below where the dirt and smoke were clearing to reveal the tangled remains of more than a dozen vehicles.

Even from here I could tell everything was worse than it

appeared. Screams echoed over to me as nurses and civilians crawled out from under the wreckage, the boxes that one of the trucks had been storing beginning to ignite. Through it all, bullets showered over everything. Whoever had set off the bombs continued their assault, even though no one that had been in the trucks had been armed.

Before I could even land, another set of bombs went off some ways away, the same buzzing electrical mass arcing over the trees. Another convoy, or maybe a village? I had no idea what they attacked, but at that point it hardly mattered. These people were not soldiers, and these people were dying.

I landed in a plume of dirt, already pulling out my phone.

Wyn. We need a med team. Kyō arrived first.

I sent it along with our coordinates, hoping it would be enough, and that people would get here in time to help.

I yelled at a few of the survivors in Ukrainian, scanning them all for my brother's face. It was mostly women, and one drunk old man in a doctor's coat.

They all looked at me with the familiar dropped jaw gape of recognition. They had seen me before, on the posters and news reports probably. But for the first time this might actually work to our benefit.

"Have you seen my brother?" I asked, realizing too late that they would have no idea of the family relation. "Have you seen the other man like me?"

They all just stared, all but one, an older lady with dark curly hair who pointed further up the caravan, where magic was now sparking.

"Thank you! Stay here, help is coming!" I yelled again as I raced away, toward the magic that I recognized as Joclyn's and Míra's.

Colors blasted through the air, sparks rippling against those same lightning bolt explosions that had ripped the caravan to shreds. The ground shook with each blast, metal groaning as whatever was causing the lightning ripped more of the cars to bits.

Weaving through the wreckage, I rushed around toppled cars and over piles of rubble in my attempt to reach them. Screams echoed in my ears as I raced past people, telling them that help was on the way.

Gripping an old side mirror on the rusted truck, I flung myself over the wreckage, coming face to face with the electrical storm that was the battle that Jos and Míra were wrapped in.

Jos and Míra, fighting Ovailia.

Except it wasn't Ovailia. She just looked remarkably like her. Long hair, stilettos, expression that looked like she was forced to keep poo in her mouth on a bet.

So much was the same. But so much was different. Starting with the electrical storm that was flying from her fingers.

I froze, watching them fight. Each woman a powerful firestorm as magic flew in every direction. Míra jumped and dodged, Jos weaved and attacked. And the Ovailia look-alike? She screamed like a mad man, letting that sparking magic fly everywhere.

Hell, she looked like a mad man with how she was raging, although that might have been because Jos and Míra were popping in and out of Stutters and forcing her into a giant game of whack-a-mole.

Fake-Ovailia screamed, turning toward where Míra had just appeared and sending a line of lightning right into where she had been.

Right into me.

"Well, shi--" Before I could even react, arms wrapped around my waist, pulling me into a few wooden crates with Míra right on top of me.

"You know, Ry," Míra quipped, pushing some of her long blonde hair behind her ear as she half-laid over me. "You might want to leave this to the girls. Not that I don't mind saving your ass."

She winked at me, and then vanished, leaving me to roll over the rumble she had tackled me onto and groan. Maybe I did want to leave this to the girls. I just watched in awe as they moved closer and closer to the woman, who grew more and more deranged until Jos was right behind her.

With just one hand to the woman's neck, Fake-Ovailia collapsed to the ground. Looking much like the rag doll that Nastya had.

"One down," Jos sighed, already looking around the rubble for the same thing I was. "And let's keep the head on this one, Míra. I have questions."

"No fun," Míra pouted, even as she turned to me and smiled.

We were nowhere near done, we still had to find my brother, but for one moment, one thing was in the right place.

Even though we still had someone else to find.

My stomach swam, my heart swelled, and I smiled back before collapsing back onto one of the boxes that had been thrown from the trucks. The wood shook from the impact, but it took me a second to realize that all of that shaking wasn't just coming from the wood.

"What the hell?" I jumped up, backing away from the box as the wood began to splinter and crack, almost like an egg.

An egg that birthed not one, but ten brightly colored Vilỳ's. Not the Vilỳ's that Edmund had poisoned and Joclyn and I had spent years hunting down, but the colorful creatures like Rinax, that bastard who had taken off before this war had even started and now flew out of the box, right to Joclyn.

"Took you long enough," he spat, his usual cranky self.

"We've been waiting for your assistance for days. Your skill with sight is clearly lacking."

Leave it to Rinax to get Joclyn raging. Her face screwed up, cheeks reddening. I half expected her to push Rinax back and scold him for vanishing. Instead, she reached out and hugged him.

I had never heard someone swear so much just for being hugged.

"Where did you come from?" she gushed, still holding on to him as he fought.

"I came from a box, you psycho, now let me go! I need to check on my kids!" She released him and he flew back to the box in a streak of blue, leaving Jos and me to stare at each other in confusion. Míra, however, was laughing like a mad woman.

"Kids?" Jos squeaked before we all raced after him to the four other Vilỳ that I had briefly seen when the box cracked under me. "What do you mean you have kids?"

"I mean I told you I was going to replenish my race and find some of my kind who were not affected by Edmund and his experiments. I found all that was left and was coming back to you when the she-bitch over there caught me." He didn't even look at us as he spoke, and was instead fluttering around each of the tiny Vilỳ in the box.

He looked like the flustered nursemaid I had when I was a toddler, which would make sense seeing as each of the creatures in the box were less than half his size and didn't appear to be any older than... well... a toddler.

"Oh my god! They are so cute!" Míra squealed coming up right beside me. I jumped at that high pitch of her voice, my magic and nerves so on edge I reacted like we were being attacked.

I wasn't the only one.

Rinax swirled around, angry little face and sharp nailed

finger pointing right in her face. "They are not cute. They are my children."

I took one step to the side to get between Míra and Rinax. Not that I thought Rinax would do anything. I grew up with him, although he was in a cage and took off the second I released him so what did I know?

"Okay, whatever you say angry man," Míra said from around me, clearly not bothered by the flying sphinx. "They are still cute."

He gave her one last look, but seemed to decide against saying anything else and soared back to the box, and to Joclyn, who was gushing just as much.

"Where did you find them?" Joclyn asked, wagging her fingers above them like she was some kind of human mobile. They cooed and reached for her fingers, one of them gnashing the horrifyingly sharp teeth that Vilỳ had. Jos didn't even seem to notice that she almost got her fingers cut off. She just kept looking at them like they were the cutest things in the world.

Weird, considering they all kind of looked like pug nosed dogs covered in slime. I passed on the chorus of 'cutes' that I was trapped in.

"I had to go to the end of the longest continent, so that I could find a tree where purple flowers sleep during the day," Rinax began, his voice just as irritated even though what he was talking about seemed like a fairytale. "I needed to coax the tree to birth the Vilỳ with an offering of snow taken from the peaks of the candy mountains where the last Xamander sleeps."

"Wow." Míra gasped the second Rinax had finished.

"You can't be serious," I groaned. None of that even made sense. There wasn't even anything called Xamander.

"Of course I'm not serious. You children are stupid and gullible." He slammed the lid back on the box of Vilỳ babies and held it out before him as he hovered in the air, blue wings fluttering violently with the effort to keep both himself and the box afloat. "I hatched them."

"I missed you Rinax," Joclyn said, patting him on the head and sending him back to scowling.

He immediately started swearing again.

16

ILYAN

BLACKNESS OVERTOOK ME. Snippets of words whispered through the black, everything rocking as my body was jostled to the side as spots of light flared in what I could have sworn was a woman's profile.

I tried to focus on it, but faded away as muffled voices yelled from a distance, the sounds garbled and broken.

"He's dangerous. Don't touch him."

"Sedate him."

"How is he still alive?"

"Isn't he the one they have been looking for?"

"I won't let you fall, Joclyn."

That last one came from inside of me.

Joclyn.

Her name was an anchor and I clung to it as I fell through the black of my sanity and back into memory. Wind tangled through my long hair, brushing over my face as long branches swayed above me.

A small robin on the branch beside me frozen in the midst of its twittering song, the leaves that surrounded him beginning to twitch before they began to rewind. The wind pulled me back as the leaves swayed in reverse. Air and memory sucked by me as I tumbled through the trees, the wind that carried me swallowing everything.

Trees pulled away from me, my arms moving awkwardly as the branches that I had propelled myself through were instead pushed away. The branches thinned before they were gone, everything moving so fast I could only make out swatches of green until I was standing right in front of her.

I would have recognized the dark hair and silver eyes anywhere, the dusting of freckles was so faint I was sure only my powerful eyes could see them. She stood before me, practically hiding behind that hair, underneath a hoodie so large she drowned in it.

This was not the woman I had seen in so many of my memories, she was not the powerful fighter that I had dreamed of for months. This was a child, a weak, whimpering thing that was one step away from running rather than accomplishing whatever task was ahead of her.

The change tangled in my gut, my muscles tensing in frustration.

Seeing her like this could have easily confused me, seeing the child and not the woman I knew. Instead, it only made me love her all the more. Knowing what she would overcome. Knowing what she would become. The emotion circled through me, the whispers of emotions and all the memories performing a kind of tango that only made my commitment to her stronger.

"I won't let you fall, Joclyn," I whispered as I stepped around her, heart tensing with the need to grab her, to hold her close. I pushed the desire away. "I promise you this above all else, I will never let anything hurt you. I am only here to protect you."

She looked to the trees in trepidation. Her silver eyes narrowed at the forest as if the plants had wronged her, somehow. The deep scowl tangled in her brow before she pulled out her bottom lip and grumbled, "Okay."

I tried not to chuckle at that, the obstinance an odd memory that I had attached to Ovailia for some reason.

Another thing I wasn't remembering.

"Now," I instructed, coming to stand behind her, "get down and prepare to jump."

My hands lifted toward her, hovering an inch away from her back in preparation to help. She moved before I could, crouching to the ground as I stood strong, the fluttering of my heart making it hard to breathe.

"Now call the wind to you," my voice was a whisper as I crouched down behind her, unable to stay far away for long.

I remained there, as close as I dared, as a powerful torrent began to whip around us, throwing hair and clothes into uncomfortable patterns.

"Now, jump."

There was the briefest hesitation, just enough to make me worry she wouldn't do it. To think that she didn't have faith in me... in herself. I jerked toward her just as she released a shaky exhale, and with one leap she soared into the air.

Her trepidation was gone as she flew, her body straightening as her arms stretched to feel the wind, as she controlled it. As she used her power.

It flowed behind her in waves, the power swelling as her magic connected to the world. As though it was the world. The strength of it in that moment made it hard to breathe.

She alone can hold your magic.

The thought filled my memory, the words followed by a swell of pride and love that was so familiar. I forced out my own shaky breath, knowing in that moment that I was witnessing more than her strength, more than her power. I was seeing a glimmer of the confidence she was hiding. I was seeing the woman she would become.

It was beautiful.

She was beautiful.

I was lost in it, until everything began to change.

I felt her magic waver before she did, the wind changing direction before she did. Jumping into the air, my own magic caught me, taking me right to her just as she began to panic. As she began to fall. Pure terror lined her face as I caught her, arms holding her close as I gave my heart and soul the thing they longed for.

Her.

Having her so close was a live wire through my veins. I pressed her into me, unable to control myself. Unable to let her go. She was here, I needed to protect her.

I would always protect her.

Bringing us to land on a tree branch, I forced out an exhale,, the reluctant motions making her stumble a bit over the tree's wide arm.

"I told you I wouldn't let you fall."

"Thank you, My Lord." She looked down, withdrawing into her hoodie as she spoke in little more than a mumble.

"I am just Ilyan now, Joclyn." I longed to step forward, to hold her again, to press her against me. But even though I knew the 'me' that was in the memory didn't know everything that was coming, he stayed still, watching her through the longing, through a pain of loss that didn't quite fit.

"Thank you, Ilyan."

It was a longing that only got worse with the sound of my name on her voice.

My name. All the need, all of the loss, all of the confusion of the last few years faded as I regained the one thing I had longed for almost more than her.

My name.

"You are very welcome." The calm of my voice didn't match the joy I felt at my name, it didn't match the desire I had to hold her against me. Still, I didn't move. "Now, we are going to do it again, but this time I want you to focus on the wind. Set your mind on what it is doing and how I am controlling it…"

These words I had heard before, on the battlefield as I launched myself into the air for the first time. The reminder of the battle swallowed the memory, the image dissipating into spots of color before it was gone altogether, leaving me staring at the black of my subconscious as I once again began to fall.

"Do not let fear enter your mind. I will be here, always." My own voice came to me through the darkness, the never-ending fall broken up by what I was sure was a soft mattress, the faint beeping I knew so well echoing through my mind and making it clear where I was.

Where I had returned.

I tried to move, to see if the restraints had returned, to prepare to fight if needed. But my body remained frozen, the steady beeping turning into a haunting metronome in my mind.

"They kept no record of him," a younger man said, his voice shaking with uncertainty, or fear judging by the snap of the man that came after.

"Either that or they took the record with them. He was important to them. That makes him important to us."

The heart rate monitor accelerated as I continued to fight against the weight my body was under. I tried to open my eyes, to tell them who I was, to ask for Kaye, to find Joclyn. Nothing happened, I lay still, trapped in darkness, listening to the sound of my heart as my lingering memories kept me company.

"I will be here always," I whispered, the words drowned by the shouts of the men and alarm as they yelled.

"He's going into cardiac arrest!"

The black swallowed me as the sound of my struggling heart faded, the ghostly whispers of the memory replacing it.

"Relax your body; do not think of the movement you are about to accomplish." The words returned in a rush of calm, the breathy whisper one that I had only heard a few times before.

The sound spun through my mind as I did through the black.

The broken fragments of my memory returned as the warmth of air and magic ran over my skin. Her skin was warm underneath mine as I placed my hands on her arms, careful not to pull her against me. She was so close.

"Focus only on the wind. Focus on its movement, on its warmth. Focus on how your magic will bring it to you. Do not worry, Joclyn; I will never let you fall" I spoke in the same breathy whisper as I gave into my need for her, pulling her against me.

The memory flickered, my heart faltering as everything sputtered back into blackness. Everything was gone but the ragged breathing and the pressure of her against me.

The feeling of empowering love faded, the emotion mutating into an unwanted anxiety as everything began to shift. The sound of the wind reduced to a low rumble that grated in my bones. It took me a moment to realize what it was, the memory falling into place.

Rocks.

Rocks that ground and slid against each other as they shifted, preparing to come down on top of us.

"I am going to blow the rest of the cave open." My snap echoed through the dark, my determination rumbling over the roar of rocks as flickers of lights began to appear, the multicolor specks feeling out of place. "I will be able to hold the ceiling for enough time for us to get to Rioseco. No matter what happens, do not stop."

"And, Joclyn?" Someone asked, the world beginning to populate as the brightly colored lights illuminated a cave, a man with long dreads shifting into view.

The man from the beach. My brother.

I had never seen him so clearly in my memory. I had never spoken to him, and yet here he was.

His face and clothes were filthy, the ratted holey things hanging off his bony frame as he stood in the middle of a cave. My brother jumped at the roar of the mountain, glancing from me, to the girl that I held in my arms. She felt different than she had in the forest. Her small frame wasn't stable, her limbs flopped around like a rag doll as I shifted her weight against me.

Her life was gone.

"I will carry her. She is my responsibility."

Rocks crashed loudly, drowning out my voice as the memory of the cave fell away, leaving me to tumble through the nothing before I froze, standing in the middle of the same black hole that had peppered the fragments of my memories.

Then there was only silence.

Only black, as I stood, the tension growing in my chest as I waited.

I didn't dare move. How could I, for all I knew one step could denote death as whatever subconscious prison I was trapped in was be shattered.

It shattered anyway, not by the sounds on my end, but by Joclyn's beautiful laugh.

The laugh cut through the tension like a knife, pulling my focus as I turned, only to come face to face with her as she smiled.

"You must choose to make the joy your focus," she said, the words jarring as she responded to the fear in my mind.

Her hair floated around her head as though she was

standing by the sea; even though it was just us standing amongst a dark nothing, only ourselves visible.

"Find happiness?" I whispered, a heavy uneasiness keeping me from moving forward.

"Yes," she sighed, the wind tugging at her, at the loose-fitting sweater she wore. The breeze was strong enough that I was sure I should feel something, yet there was nothing. "It's a choice, isn't it? Have you chosen to be happy, Ilyan?"

The weak girl who soared through the trees was gone, but so was the powerful woman I had spent so many beachside dreams with. The way she smiled, the way she glanced at me... It couldn't be her, and yet, I could feel something deep inside of me pull towards her, scream for her.

"Joclyn?"

She smiled, pushing more hair out of her face as she took a tentative step forward.

"You have to choose to be happy," she said, the unfamiliar glance digging deep. "If you don't choose joy, you will never experience it."

"That sounds familiar." My voice was a little more than a gasp as some memory tried to pull its way out of the pit of my subconscious, only the whisper of an older man made its way through.

"Dramin would say that to you for decades while you waited for her," she paused, her eyes focused far past me and into the blackness that surrounded us. "He would say it to Joclyn..."

"To Joclyn," I interrupted her, her focus pulling to me as an unfamiliar smile threatened the corners of her mouth. "But aren't you..?"

"You know that I am not," she said, that same foreign smile twitching around the corners of her mouth, "Your soul has already told you as much."

For years I had known that the Joclyn I lay on the beach with was just a fabrication, but she was so similar to the girl from my dreams that I never questioned it was her.

But this woman had stolen the woman I loved so much and invaded my mind. I wanted to destroy her, to rip her apart and cast her into the darkness.

I could feel my temper growing, the need to destroy her growing. There was something else there, however, that stopped me. Something that was drawing me to her.

"Who are you?"

"I am part of you, the part that is missing," she spoke in a singsong voice, like the words were a riddle. Although I was sure the words were meant to help, they only befuddled me more. My quickly growing urgency for who she was made it hard for me to see the possibility in the words.

Wait.

What.

What she was, not who.

My eyes narrowed as hers widened as if she knew what was coming.

"What are you?"

Her smile brightened as she stepped forward, that same internal battle raging over, pulling away, and rushing closer. Instead, I stood still, fingers clenching and unclenching against the tense muscles in my thighs.

"That is the right question." Her hair continued to blow in the wind, tangling over the bright silver eyes that bored into me. Although she was less than a foot from me, I still felt nothing.

Not even a whisper of the breeze.

My heart rampaged, pulling for her. Needing her. The emotion was familiar, but it was not the love I felt for Joclyn.

It was not the same.

This was a hunger.

The feeling was feral, like I was an animal that needed to

take possession of this woman. Possession of whatever she was. The unwanted need twisted in my gut and I stepped away from her, her smile falling as her eyes flashed darkly.

"Why don't you want me?" she asked, the danger in her eyes growing further. "You have been searching for me, haven't you? I am right here, Ilyan."

"You are not Joclyn." I was surprised by the hostility in my own voice.

"I know." Her coy response only flared my anger more.

"I have been searching for my..." I stalled.

The word that fit Joclyn was lost. I could feel it there, the memory waiting for me.

"For your what?" she taunted, the haunting anger beginning to fade as she teased. "For your wife? Your mate?"

My heart was a thunder. It beat against my ribs painfully as the memory I had seen before of me braiding her hair replayed in my mind. The image made no sense, but it didn't matter. I knew she was telling the truth. She was my wife. My mate. This memory was the moment she became that.

No wonder I longed for her, she was my other half.

"No, she is more than that," the imposter said, the abrupt answer to my thoughts pulling me out of my memories.

The woman's eyes sparkled now, all sign of her temper from before gone. "She is the other part of your soul."

"My soul," I repeated, the knot in my chest constricting as she once again stepped closer, my heart battling again with both need and frustration. "That is what you are. You are my soul."

It wasn't a question. I was certain. It didn't get the reaction I had expected, however.

"No." Any sign of a smile was gone now, her jaw was tight, her words sinking into me as much as her stare. "I am more important than that."

I could only stare at her, keeping the rocks of my fists against my thighs as she stepped closer, her hair and clothing blowing and flapping in the ethereal wind.

"I am not really enjoying this game you are playing," I growled, finally taking a step away from her.

"Aren't you?" I wasn't sure if she was playing or pushing, but it didn't matter. The way she looked at me still sparked loud and clear.

"No." The single word was little more than a growl. "Tell me what you are."

No matter how much I longed for whatever this imposter was, she was still just that. I didn't want her here.

"But you are enjoying the way you want me, the way you are screaming for me..."

"You are not Joclyn!" I roared, the anger that she had been prodding finally breaking free. Instead of stepping back, however, she grinned. A laugh threatening to break free as she reached toward me again.

"No, I am your magic."

The anger froze.

My breath froze.

Everything held still, except for the invisible wind that tumbled through her hair.

"I am all that is left of your magic from when you died." She stepped closer, but this time I couldn't step away, I could barely breathe.

When I died.

I had always known. I had focused so much on that bloodstained wall in the beginning. I knew what it was.

"Explain." The single word whispered in a gasp.

"You died that night in the cave, and your sister sacrificed herself to rectify a wrong." She stalled, her words hitting hard as a million sparks of memories began to make sense. "She chose to rectify a lifetime of wrongs."

"Ovailia." Saying her name was a pain in my heart, a physical stab that twisted against my soul, one piece of the puzzle suddenly making sense.

"You have lived without your memories long enough, but I wonder what you would choose, given the chance?"

She paused, stepping away from me for the first time. Instead of relaxing at the motion, however, I tensed, scared I was going to lose her.

"The chance..."

"If I could return your memories right now," she interrupted, turning her back on me as a tiny spark of white light erupted deep into of the black. "Would you take them over your magic? Would you sacrifice power for the knowledge of who you are?"

"Which will take me to Joclyn?"

"To your wife?" she clarified, still looking toward the light that was now bright enough to frame her in a yellow glow.

"Yes. Which will take me to my wife." My heart fluttered at the word on my tongue, the emotion swelling comfortably and I sighed.

"Neither." The word was a stab in my heart. "One will give you knowledge, but take away your power to reach her. The other will give you power, but you will not know where to find her."

The eyes of the imposter grew dark, the entire surface plunging into the abyss as she stared into me. The glow from behind her dimmed as she lifted her hands, one cradling the fist of the other as the light began to seep through her closed fingers.

I stared at the light, my body filled with both familiarity and need, that same feral emotion now desperate to jump on her, to take whatever she held and reclaim it as my own.

"I told you I am small. I am all that is left of a power that was once a great flood." She opened her hand.

The light that I had seen behind her was condensed into a pebble in the palm of her hand.

"I am not strong enough anymore," she whispered, closing her hand over the light.

My hand jerked toward the light, desperate to grab it. It was a small motion, but the woman noticed, smiling at me sadly as she once again stepped closer, her hand held between us as lines of light spread from below.

"You must find Joclyn, Ilyan," she pleaded as she opened her hand again. The light swelled into the dark, lifting from her palm as it began to pulse with the tiniest fade. "She is your mate, she holds your magic safe. She is the only one who can return what was lost, who can bring back your memories, who can return you to who you once were."

Her words were a mumble in the back of my mind, my focus still on the light, on the way it pulsed, on the way it called to me...

"Ilyan," she said, her voice a roar. "You must find her."

"How am I supposed to find someone that I can barely remember?" I didn't even try to keep the gruff desperation from flooding my words.

"Do you choose to remember then?" The question caught me off guard.

Instead of answering, I just stared at her, jaw working as I looked at her and the tiny pebble of magic that hovered above my head. My heart pulled and ached with a need, two separate desires; one fueled in desperation, one fueled by passion.

I could feel them both. But only one scared me to possess. Only one scared me to lose.

"I wish to find my wife." Referring to her as what she was to me was a breath of fresh air. "I would die to see her one last time. To hold her in my arms. To remember her."

The imposter smiled, the light in her eyes shining so

brightly that for one moment I was sure it was Joclyn, that I had gotten my wish and she had been returned to me.

It was only a mirage.

The wind around her picked up as she opened her hand between us, the tiny ball of light flew back into her hand, pulsing between us again. The rhythm suddenly made sense.

The pulse of a heart.

As I watched it, however, I knew that it was not my heart. The beat was not mine, it was not the phantom that stood before me.

It was hers.

"Joclyn," I gasped, my fingers floating toward the orb again.

"Joclyn will return your magic. She will return your power. I will give you the memories I have of her. Of your life."

"Wait..." I tried to interrupt.

"They are the keys to finding the other half to your soul," she continued on, ignoring me. "But you must hurry. You are an Ancient, I am not sure what a loss of your magic will do to you. I do not know how you will fare once I am gone."

"Where are you going?"

"I am giving myself to you," she whispered, lifting her hand up toward me, streams of light flooding through the tiny gaps in her fingers.

The ribbons of light streamed over us, but this time the shadows on her face were not filled with the same beauty and hunger as they had been before. This time there was a sadness there, a pain that I could feel infecting me, seeping through me like a cold shower.

The pain left as she opened her hand, flooding us with light and bringing back the feral need in a groan that ripped from my chest.

"I am giving you all that I have, all that I am, so that you can find her. So that you can find yourself, so that you can return me to what I truly am. So that you can be what you truly are." Her voice was so soft I had to strain to hear her, the emotion, the pain, growing as she stepped even closer, her hand almost touching my chest.

"My magic..."

"For your memories," she interrupted me with a paralyzing gasp, the pain rampaging through her and right into me.

"How can I reach her if I don't have my magic? I am not even sure if I am alive." A different kind of fear racked through me, a genuine terror that I didn't know how to compute.

It was my magic that had kept me alive for years, that had continued to heal me as I was tortured. I didn't know what awaited me outside of my dreams, outside of my memories. I didn't know if I could survive it without that power.

"You are alive," she gasped, her free hand lifting toward me, her flat palm hovering inches from my shoulder, so close I swear I could feel her make contact. "You are safe. Your body is healed."

"How do you know that?"

"You must find your mate, Ilyan." I was well aware that she was not answering my question, but it didn't matter. I trusted her.

"She will reignite the power, she will bring your strength back when you find her. But you have to find her."

"I will."

"Find your mate, Ilyan," she whispered, tears flowing down her cheeks. "She is waiting for you."

She looked at me one last time, the deep silver in her eyes glinting before she slammed her hand into my chest, pressing the bright light into the skin that spread over my heart.

A pain as though I had been stabbed rippled over my skin, rattling my bones as agony spread over me. I looked down in horror, expecting to see my chest covered in blood. Instead, each of the scars that criss-crossed over my chest was glowing with the same light that had beamed from her hand.

"What..."

"Find her, Ilyan." Her words were like wind, the syllables swept away as if she was nothing more than dust. "Find her."

"I will find her." I gasped, the words as breathy as the air that rattled around me.

The force of the wind grew as I fell into the space around me, power and magic dragging me through nothing.

Nothing but black.

"I will find her," I said, my voice an odd gasp when the falling stopped, as the world changed, to a mattress cradling my body.

And I opened my eyes to a vase of freshly cut flowers.

17

ILYAN

The flowers were fresh.

I could smell them from where I lay on yet another hospital bed. I could see each fleck of pollen on the low hanging stamens. See the detail on the tiny drops of dew that covered the petals. I stared at the bright red petals as wide beams of light fell over them, the unfamiliar beauty streaming from the white-curtained windows to a cracked stone floor.

The stone was similar to what I had used in the bathrooms in Rioseco, it had taken me months to find the perfect....

My breath caught, my body tensing under the soft cotton blankets as a heart rate monitor somewhere in the room began to speed up.

Rioseco. The Abbey I had built as a safe haven. The Abbey I had taken Joclyn to.

I remembered.

I remembered everything.

The monitors sped even faster as I sat up, the blanket falling away to reveal a mess of wires and tubes and who knows what else attached to my skin and inserted into my arms.

I waved my hand, expecting them all to fall away with one

surge of power. But nothing happened. Each tube remained plunged into arms, wires to chest.

I growled, the memory of the imposter from my dream slamming hard against my chest as my heart did. Magic for my memories.

At least, with the limited knowledge that I had, I had chosen my memories. I had chosen my Joclyn.

"I'm coming, my love." My voice was scratchy and coarse from ill-use, but the word, the phrase, the language, was so missed, so longed for, that it was followed by a sigh anyway.

I was coming. And I knew right where to go.

She would be in Imdalind, and if I had gotten out of Ukraine I could be there in days.

I moved to stand, my head spinning with the movement just as the door to my room opened. I turned at the sound, expecting to see Kaye walking in. Instead of the boisterous brunette, however, it was a young Asian man with oversized spectacles that only exaggerated the look of horror he had at seeing me sitting there.

"What has happened?" the man stuttered in Mandarin, his eyes darting behind him as he began to back out of the room.

"Where have I been taken?" I asked in the same language, the shock and fear on his face growing as he took another step, mouth opening to yell at someone behind him. "I mean you no harm, if you could hel..."

"The monster is awake!" he screamed as he stepped back, slamming the door behind him and leaving me staring at the dark slab of wood.

Yells and shouts filtered through the heavy wooden door, the word 'monster' repeated over and over. Well, that didn't work.

"Hovno," I swore loudly, the word felt awkward without the surge of power behind it.

I didn't have much time. The screams grew louder as my

heart rate increased, the beeping turning into a high pitched squeal as I began to rip off the sticky pads that covered my chest. Multiple monitors flatlined before my fingers wrapped around the tubes inserted into my arms. The cold tubing pumped gently underneath my fingers, the pulse was as quick as my heart.

Whatever it was had clearly been inserted directly into a vein. Judging by the size of the tube, if I just ripped it out I would have more problems than my blood splashed over flowers.

I couldn't heal.

Although there was a shadow of magic deep inside of me, it wasn't responding, I wasn't even sure if it was magic. For all I knew, all mortals felt this way.

I stood, everything spinning again as I searched for a cloth or something to apply pressure so I could remove the tube. I was barely able to grip the nightstand beside the bed before I tumbled back down, the spinning overtaking me.

Screw healing, I couldn't even fight like this.

It didn't matter either way, head still spinning, tubing still pumping, the door was thrown open and a line of soldiers walked in, guns drawn.

Scooting back against the headboard, the line of muzzles grew closer, the mumblings of what sounded like Russian, Mandarin, and even English buzzing from the hall.

"I mean you no harm," I said the words on repeat, moving through every language I was hearing and even adding a few others that were colloquially similar.

The men and women behind the guns began to look at each other, their eyes wide with the same fear that the man who had walked in before had.

It made sense as to why.

Although I had no idea if any of these soldiers were the ones who had shot me, I had a feeling the last thing they had been told was a story of me soaring through the air, firing infantile magic at people.

I thought I had been so powerful, so strong. The memory caused me to shake my head. If I had my memories, if I had control of even the tiny bit of magic I had retained I could have been out of here months after they had found me in the alley.

"Where is Kaye," I said clearly in Ukrainian, the switch from my language tour taking a few of the soldiers off guard.

"I do not know what you mean."

I jerked at the clear voice, the English heavily accented with what was clearly Russian. Although the voice itself was not familiar, the tone, the words were filled with enough ice that my magic's promise that I was safe seemed foolhardy.

"Where is Kaye," I repeated the words in English, eliminating as much of my own accent as I could while keeping my voice strong.

"Is this a person?" the same voice responded. Even the soldiers that surrounded my bed were shifting in unease. "Is this the woman from the massacre in Prague?"

I focused on keeping my breathing even, on keeping my face impassive as I stared at the soldiers, the row of unfamiliar uniforms still shielding whoever was talking.

"We believe you are the man from that attack," he continued on after a moment of silence. "Is this true?"

Oh great. We were starting over.

"I do not know what you are talking about." My voice was much harder than it should have been. I shifted my weight, leaning toward the voice. "Kaye is my nurse."

The wall of blast guards and gun tips stared me down, the hidden faces of the soldiers looking at me with eyes so wide I began wondering if something else had changed since our attempted escape.

It was not the soldiers that were concerning, however, it was the man who emerged from among them, his lanky frame leaning against the foot of my bed.

The blonde man curled his hands around the metal railing as he leaned toward me, the military uniform diminishing his frame somehow. I had never met him before, but that hardly mattered. I knew the look, I knew the posturing voice.

All of these men were the same.

I would have to be tricky. At least I didn't have handcuffs to deal with this time.

"You are looking for your nurse?" he asked, the confusion growing at my request.

"She was my friend." I was successful in keeping the frustration out of my voice that time. "Where is she?"

"Do you mean the woman you tried to escape from the SSU with? The leader of the villagers?"

I remained quiet. Although we both got what we wanted even without my confirmation.

"This is not the SSU," I said.

His eyes sparked at my statement, lip twitching as his hands tightened against the railing.

"We are part of the republic." His tone made it clear he wasn't going to say any more. He didn't need to. I knew little of The Republic of the Kyō, looking at the nationalities of those who surrounded me, however, I had less information than I thought.

"And where is this republic? Russia?" I asked.

The man said nothing, he only smiled, a torturous joy taking hold. It wasn't him that I was looking at, however, it was the soldiers on either side of him.

The two men were clearly Asian, although from where I could not tell. Judging by the disdain that came over their face at my question, we were clearly not in Russia.

Russia was here.

So, maybe China. If I had to guess I would say we were somewhere in the high mountains of Mongolia.

The room itself bore no sign of that, the furniture, the medical equipment, everything about it screamed of western Europe. The long curtains, however, and the fresh flowers that were cut in the vase were little hints to the culture that this smothering Russian was hiding.

I had spent time in Mongolia several hundred years before, and while I knew the terrain, it was remote enough that without the aid of my power I could not escape it easily.

"It does not matter where you are," the man sneered, his accent growing deeper. "Now that you are awake you will be moved back to more... familiar... surroundings."

His smile grew and my gut twisted uncomfortably, his tone enough to detail what was waiting for me.

"Unless of course, you choose to work with us," he prompted, the light of eagerness returning. "Unless you choose to join us."

I hesitated, muscles and jaw tightening. Our eyes locked in an intense stare as the soldiers began to shift their weight, the muzzles of their guns moving to a tighter aim.

The tension of the room increased with each moment that passed, the simple task of getting back to Joclyn becoming more impossible.

"What do you want to know?"

Keeping my hands tight against the mattress I let my eyes wander to the soldiers, searching for any gap or weakness. When I looked back to the Russian he was beaming with an eagerness he wasn't even trying to hide.

"I want to know everything," he said, his greediness a snake that twisted around my gut. "You see, we know who you are. We know what you can do. And while we have an idea of what the

SSU has discovered of you, all of their research was lost when they fell. When Nastya was killed."

I would have celebrated that, if her death had actually led to my release and not just another prison.

He hesitated, tapping against the rail on the bed as he took a step back, studying me as I had him before he leaned forward, the simple action twisting my stomach into my chest.

"We wish to learn of you," he continued, the look in his eyes causing the muscles in my emaciated back to tense. "We wish to recreate you. And we do not wish to resort to the same procedures as your former captors."

It was the same. They were all the same.

I was like a shiny toy to all of them, the power inside of me one that they wanted for themselves. Except now there was no power inside of me, there was no magic. And if he resorted to the same techniques that Nastya had, there would be no tomorrow.

No Joclyn.

My heart twisted uncomfortably, my stomach growing warm at the thought of her, at the possibility of losing her. I pushed the fearful emotion aside and looked at the Russian straight on, keeping my jaw tight in my wavering defiance.

"The power that you seek is no longer with me," I said honestly, the few words tangling painfully in my gut. I felt the same warmth at my admission, felt the tension in my chest, but no more than that. There was no flood of strength, there was no electric rumbling, there was nothing but a mortal body.

He smiled, a single chuckle scratched through the air before he tapped his fingers against the rail and began to pace. The soldiers made way for him, their focus still on me.

"I do not need to show you the images that say otherwise," he said, rocking on his toes as he stepped closer to me. "You know of them."

I did, and while I had told him the truth, he was not willing to listen. As much as he wished for my cooperation, I would have to resort to the story he wished for.

"I have told them before, I do not remember..."

"This is not the SSU," the man interrupted, attempting to hide his impatience with flattery. "You do not have to hide truths from us."

I looked from the Russian to the natives that surrounded me, their fingers twitching as they held their guns to me in restrained horror.

"I see no difference between this and the SSU," I said, transitioning my words into a smooth Czech, that I could tell only he understood. "It is the same threats, the same danger."

His frustrations boiled with each word until they exploded, his very body began to shake as he spoke with a clear, concise, fury. "We are not the SSU..."

"Yes, you are the Kyō," I filled in for him, my calm defiance setting him off further. Both his patience and control were wavering.

"Yes." The grind of the word made it clear he wasn't going to say more.

"What is the Kyō," I queried, careful to keep my voice light lest I push him even further.

The man said nothing, he only tightened his jaw, struggling to keep his own control.

"If I do not know what you are, how can I trust you?"

The question stopped the man dead in his tracks and while the smile that I had seen before was clearly still present, it was there for a different reason.

"You are not in a place to be given trust," he said, the wickedness back in his eyes as he nodded once, the soldiers shifting as a reminder of the control he had, no matter how much his emotions attempted to push him otherwise.

"Then I am not in a place to tell you everything you ask."

The man's pride bristled, his eyes glancing toward the soldiers for the first time before he tapped his heels, the frustration rippling off him.

"If you tell me nothing, then I cannot help you."

I stared at him as he leaned over the rail, waiting for something more, waiting for something to click. There nothing there but a desperation I didn't understand, however, something about him that didn't quite fit with the scene I was surrounded by.

Something was wrong.

"If I tell you everything, how will I know I will be alive by morning?" I asked as a younger soldier caught my focus, his eyes wide with fear as he looked right into me.

Sweat dripped down the soldiers' brow, the muzzle of his gun shaking the tiniest bit. His finger clearly compressing the trigger.

"Or is there nothing you can do?"

The Russians focus pulled right to the soldier at my question, his eyes obviously catching what I had.

The guns were empty.

The room, everything, it was all a facade.

"Put him on the next transport," he growled, his Mandarin barely understandable through the clench in his teeth.

The soldiers around us looked between themselves in obvious fear before the man began to scream again, switching between Ukrainian, Russian, and Mandarin so fast I wasn't sure anyone besides he and I could follow.

"Do it now!" the man continued to roar, his face turning purple in his anger.

It was the last thing I saw before the butt of a gun intersected with my temple and, magic or not, I was plunged back into the world of dreams.

18

WYN

"I'm starting to think I need to build a room just for interrogating people. Maybe I can build it off the main hall, a little stone room where we can ask people why they like killing others so much." We had never needed a prison before this, but seeing as we now had not one but two people wrapped in my fire chains, it was becoming a bit of a necessity.

Thankfully there hadn't been any more need in all of the survivors we had brought back. There were at least sixty that we had pulled out of the wreckage of the hospital and the caravan that Jos, Míra, and Ryland had been in. We had found another caravan that had taken the same hit closer to the border, but no one had been alive there.

Most of those who had returned were nurses and other Chosen that Nasty woman had been experimenting on. They had been locked away by the SSU for so long they didn't seem sure about what to think of us.

"Spoken like a true assassin. Hurt first, ask questions later." I whirled around to the bright blue flying rat that Joclyn and Ryland had found. Rinax.

He had been an unexpected find. Him, along with the

Ovailia look-a-like that was chained to a bed alongside the other would-be assassin. That, combined with the recovering Míra, should have made their escape into the SSU a success. But they hadn't found Ilyan.

All you had to do was look at Jos to see the devastation there. She was hiding it, but everything about her looked like it was going to 'plode'. The only question was: in or out.

No wonder Ryland was standing so close to her. I was just as close, but that was mostly just to keep me from ringing Rinax's neck. Thom was off terrorizing children, so there was no one else to stop me.

"That's where you are wrong," I snapped, rounding on the sourpuss who just sat scowling at us all. "If I was killing everyone first I wouldn't need to ask questions."

"I said hurt not kill--!"

"Rinax," Jos sighed, cutting him off, and sending the little ball of fury sputtering again.

You would think after he took off and vanished for over three years he would have found a better attitude, especially considering he had returned with a handful of Vilỳ that weren't poisoned. But nope, he was still a little ball of rage.

"We will address all murdering later, but for now," Jos waved her hands, my chains shifting on the Ovailia look alike they had brought, "we have a mystery on our hands."

We all took a step closer to her. She didn't even flinch.

"Who are you? Because we all know you aren't Ovailia," Jos said, and thankfully the woman didn't yell or scream like the other one was still doing. She hadn't really stopped attempting to get out of the chains since I put her in them last night.

"Ovailia." She spoke the name slowly, like she was having trouble getting her mouth around it. When she did speak it was in perfect English. It caught me off guard. "Is that her name? The woman I've been pretending to be? I never knew. I just had them all use my name. It was easier that way."

Ryland stiffened, Jos's magic flaring in confusion. Hell, we were all confused, even the SSU's assassin had stopped her ceaseless screaming to stare.

"Oh, don't look at me like that," she continued, giving the woman next to her a look. "You too, Dinah, don't you dare act like this world isn't cutthroat. I was given a chance to live, so I took it. My name is Ivory by the way." She grinned as she looked from the now named Dinah to Jos, her grin spreading into something so malicious that even my spine straightened. "And you are The Oheň."

"I'm so tired of that nickname," Jos sighed, leaning against the footboard as she clearly played into the twisted hunger on Ivory's face. "It's more suited to her," she waved a hand to me. "She *actually* catches on fire."

"It's true." I clicked my tongue and bounced on my heels. If I couldn't get a cool nickname, maybe I would just steal Jos's. "I control fire."

I snapped my fingers for dramatic effect and set both sets of chains on fire for a second, just enough to set Dinah screaming before I extinguished them.

"Now, really, do we have to be so childish?" Rinax scoffed, his wings clicking together in irritation. No one even turned to look at him.

"My name is Joclyn," Jos continued, giving each of them a nod. "And just in case you are wondering, as I am sure you are, Ovailia is actually my sister-in-law."

I repressed a giggle. It was true, as far as human titles went anyway. But in this case Ovailia being her step-mother was also true, and very weird. Ryland gave me a look. Right, we were supposed to be ominous.

"Ah, so she is the sister of the blond man in those pictures."

Jos stiffened at the statement, the air suddenly becoming very heavy as Ivory looked between us, realizing what she had hit on.

Ivory was grinning with the same malicious grin as before, the twisted smile pulling all of my magic right to the surface. We tested her, and no one found any magic in her, but I wasn't about to count her out as an enemy just because of that.

She looked at Joclyn like she wanted to cut her up and take a picture of what was inside.

"Ah, he is the one I am assuming you showed up at the hospital to find. And how about the little blonde girl? Your daughter? So we had your family, and you just missed them..." Ivory grinned more, Dinah laughing hysterically from behind the chains that covered her mouth. She sounded like a deranged clown.

"We didn't miss them." Ryland's voice was a deep roar as he stepped forward, staring each of them down in turn. He didn't elaborate any more, content to let them think what they wanted. Ivory looked shocked for half a second before she settled back into her chains, still smiling.

"Well, you will have to ask Jan how he liked pretending not to know you all those years, then. He put on a great show, even when we removed his arms he still didn't break. We never found you. Glad to know you found him in the end so that you could be reunited. What's left of him anyway. Poor guy didn't even know what way was up after all the experiments I ran on him."

The chains flew off of Ivory so fast I couldn't have stopped them if I tried. For half a second I thought she had revealed her magic and was attacking, both Ryland and I going into fight mode, magic at the ready.

But, she wasn't attacking. She couldn't even move as Joclyn stepped forward, her magic wrapped around her as she threw her to the ceiling with such force that cracks began to web over the surface behind her, the thin lines growing the harder Joclyn compressed her into the ceiling.

"I didn't... what are... how could..." Ivory couldn't get out more than a few words with the pressure Joclyn was placing on her. I could have sworn I heard more than two ribs crack over the sound of Dinah's screams and Ivory's sobs.

"What did you do to him?" I jumped at the voice, the low menacing growl so volatile it didn't even sound like Joclyn. Hell, she didn't even look like Joclyn.

Her skin was pale, almost as though it had been drained of color. The near white of her skin only made her eyes creepier. They were the black of sight as she stepped below where Ivory was now embedded in the ceiling, her magic flew around the room, sending hair and clothes whipping.

Ivory tried to answer, or maybe just laugh at her, but I don't think Joclyn was really asking. She held a mug in one hand, her fingers dipped below the surface of the amber liquid before her magic sparked again and she soared the seven feet into the air to reach her, placing her Black Water covered fingers against her cheeks.

Ivory screamed, Dinah screamed, and Rinax sighed like he was bored. I turned, and sure enough he sat with his head in one hand while he inspected the nails of the other.

He only looked up with interest when Joclyn began speaking with the low rumble of sight. He saw me looking at him, however, and darted his hands back to his nails.

"In the high mountains. Far from the plains. In the islands, against the land. Find them marching. Defeat the fire. Take the source. Repair the land."

I looked at Ryland, but he was staring at Joclyn, at the way her body began to shake. Damn it. All that rage and she was going to snap the woman in two if she wasn't careful. Ivory was still sputtering on the ceiling, the burn of the Black Water now spreading over her arm.

"I'll take Ivory, you grab Jos?" I asked, and Ryland didn't hesitate, he rushed forward, cutting Joclyn's magic off as he pulled her back. Jos was still so deep in sight that I wasn't even sure she noticed he was dragging her out of the room.

I grabbed Ivory before she hit the ground, my magic rough as it shoved her back on the bed and wrapped my heavy chains around her again.

"What... what... was that?" Ivory gasped out, staring at the door that Ryland had pulled Joclyn through.

"That? Oh, that is the power of the Drak. The Queen, and the woman whose mate you just confessed to torturing, is the last living Drak. You may have lived this long by pretending to be someone else, but your luck just ran out." I grinned at her, leaning against the foot of the bed as I too inspected my nails in feigned boredom.

I could have sworn I heard Rinax snicker from behind me. Okay, so this he enjoyed.

"Did you really think that would go another way?" Rinax snickered, flying down to land on the metal railing by my hands. "If the Queen didn't hurt you, I would. You hurt me and my children, too."

Ivory tried to sputter a response, but Rinax cut her off.

"She has been pretending to be Ovailia," Rinax began, clearly knowing more about her than she thought. The second Rinax detailed out what he knew her eyes grew to massive pools of panic. "The Kyō found her first, then the SSU. They thought they recognized her from the posters and wanted to find out what made her tick, except she didn't have magic..."

"That's not what happened," Ivory said with a laugh, like she was some kind of villain ready to monologue and wasn't just a mortal with a death wish tied to a bed. Dinah yelled something in terror, but Ivory didn't even turn. "Oh shut up, Dinah. The SSU has fallen. These guys will be next, then it won't matter what I say."

"God, what is it with these overconfident bastards with their crappy magic thinking they can take us on?" It was really starting to get on my nerves.

"We can take you on."

"Thank you for proving my point." I rolled my eyes, but she just grinned and tried to lean forward, the chains rattling before I tightened them and sent her right back into the headboard.

"We have been harvesting magic--"

"Yes, we know. The Kyō have been siphoning it off the Chosen for electricity. The SSU have been taking it for those stupid guns. I wasn't there to see what the SSU did, but those two were." I knocked my head back to the door and to the hall where Jos and Ry were hissing at each other. That must have been some sight. "And based on what you said you helped make all those creepy instruments to do it, and--" I glanced to the door. Jos was really not going to like this if I was right. "*Jan* was your guinea pig to make it all work."

I couldn't tell if Ivory was pissed as hell, or impressed at my quick deduction, not that she had made it all that hard. Either way, her expression was amazing and I laughed, tapping my short painted nails against the bed rail.

"Is there anything I missed?" I asked, even though I had all the information we needed, including the name they had given Ilyan, who apparently didn't remember any of us. No wonder he hadn't just come rushing back three years ago.

"Did I miss anything?" I asked again, looking from Ivory, to Rinax, to the still shouting Dinah. "No?"

Still no answer. Nothing but blank stoic stares that were almost worse given the continued conversation between Ryland

and Jos. Damn. I really needed to get out there. Jos had clearly seen something.

"Okay, then." I gave her a smile and tightened both of their chains before I turned to the door. It was only when my hand was on the knob that I spoke.

"What about where he is?" Ivory sputtered in what she clearly thought was victory. I turned, surprised to see Rinax still perched on the metal rail of the foot of the bed, smiling just as widely as I was.

"Well, I've already told you," he squeaked, "the Queen is a Drak. Which means she can see into your past and your future. You've been in direct contact with our King, which means you might have just been the key we needed. We will find him, and then you will be tried."

Poor Ivory clearly thought she had the upper hand. She just stared at us with her jaw hanging down to her lap as we left. Even Rinax smiled at her before we closed the door.

"I highly suggest you lock that door and forget what was inside," Rinax whispered the second the door was closed. "That woman, in the wrong hands, would do more damage than Ovailia ever could."

I couldn't help but think he was right.

19

RYLAND

"YOU CAN'T KILL HER." I was firm, but Joclyn wasn't having it.

"No one will miss her." Anger was radiating off her, and I already knew I was going to have a hard time getting her to calm down. Not after what she told me she saw. Nastya torturing Ilyan, and the woman on the other side of the door making the machines that did it.

"Still not a good reason to murder someone."

"But what she did, Ry, I--" I put my hands on her arms, our gazes locked as I held her only a few inches away from me. She tried to dodge me, but I moved faster, refusing to let her look away.

"She will pay, but let's not let Rinax be right. The little guy drives me batty, but he's right. Enough people will die over all of this. Enough people already have."

"And what about the ones who deserve it?" she hissed, her magic sparking through my hands as she yanked her arms away from me. I inhaled sharply as the icy blast of her magic hit me.

"You mean the ones who are guilty?" I clarified, but she only narrowed her eyes at me. "Let Ilyan decide, the crimes are against him, yes? Let him decide *when* we bring him home."

All of her defiant energy seemed to sizzle, the bright spark in her silver eyes fading as she inhaled, the slow, steady breath lingering behind us.

"When," she repeated, but it was not a question. From what she told me, she had seen enough to find him. We may not have found him in Ukraine, but now it was only a matter of time. "My sight showed mountains. And it showed the Kyō. So my guess is that they have him."

"So high mountains... in probably China or Japan. Mongolia maybe?" I tried to remember what little I had retained from high school geography class. I traveled a lot of places throughout my father's insane quest to kill my brother, but I had never gone to either of those places.

It would figure that my quest to bring him home would be the reason for me to go there.

"Based on what little I saw, my money would be on Mongolia. So, we need to find a medical station in the high mountains. A needle in a haystack." She sounded so dejected, so broken.

"A lot of space, but there aren't going to be many large medical centers in the middle of nowhere, Jos."

"True." She took another long inhale, taking some of the stress that was in the air with it. "They probably aren't going to keep him somewhere away from their main complex either. We find him, we find whatever snake is at the head of that beast."

"And then we finish this." It felt good to say that, even if we both knew that was nowhere near the end.

"Well, until we let Wyn take her crown as Empress Supreme and it all goes to hell again." She grinned, both of us laughing at the ridiculousness of it. Part of me actually thought Wyn would be a good ruler. The other part was scared about just how much she would burn to the ground, especially with how crabby she had been lately.

"We may not have found Ilyan, but our trip to Ukraine was still worth it." I grabbed her arms again, ready to pull her into a hug if she was going to collapse again. But she just stood there smiling at me, her hand soft as she placed it against my arm.

"For you too." Oh god, I knew that look. It was the same one Wyn had given me. Jos may have been oblivious before, but she knew now.

"Fucking Thom." I suddenly felt the need to slam my fist into the wall. She just laughed.

"Yeah, it's like he's excited for you or something." She rolled her eyes and slugged me in the shoulder. Same as she always had. "Now go check on Míra. I'm going to go get a team started on scouring upper Mongolia."

Jos smiled and raced off, if she wasn't trying to be all queenly right then she probably would have been skipping. As her second I technically should be following her. But she was right, I was already being pulled in another direction.

I knocked once when I reached Míra's room, the muffled 'come in' sounded a bit too much like the angsty teenager who liked to destroy her room and my heart dropped as I opened the door. Her room wasn't in shambles, however, she just sat on her bed, wearing a pair of fuzzy pajama pants and a matching shirt as she stared at the two torn pieces of paper in her hands.

I recognized them immediately: the letter she had left for me. I was pretty sure my stomach turned into a swarm of angry bees.

Nervous energy rippled through me as she looked up and promptly shoved the pieces of paper under her leg, clearly trying to make everything look as normal as possible. I was pretty sure it wasn't going to be possible with the bit of damp in her eyes and how my entire being seemed ready to burst through my skin and run away.

"How are you doing?" I asked, foolishly stumbling on each

and every word as I stepped into the room and let the door swing shut behind me.

"I'm showered and wearing clean clothes for the first time since I almost died, so I think it's safe to say I'm doing hunky-dory." She swung her arm over waist like some old timey dancer. "How did interrogating the fake Ovailia go?"

That was one way to quickly dampen my nerves. "About as well as interrogating a bear. I guess they just confused her for Ovailia in all those pictures from when the zit popped and she went along with it. Made the guns and the electricity machines."

"So your garden-variety villainess." She forced a laugh, shifting her weight as I moved closer in an obvious attempt at hiding the note better. "Oh the mountains I could have climbed if I hadn't switched sides."

Another laugh, this one accompanied by a forced smile as I sunk into the bed next to her.

"I read your note." I used to be so much better at being debonair. I had lost some of that while being tortured, and the rest while being used as bait. Now I was just a tactless weirdo. Míra blinked at me, those tears she had been trying to hide coming right back to the surface. I was off to a great start.

"Did you tear it up?" She pulled the two pieces out from where she had hidden them and I nodded, realizing a second too late what exactly I had done.

"Oh! I did, but not like that. I was just so excited to see it, I opened it too fast and..." I mimed my overexuberant paper opening and subsequent ripping, which mostly just looked like I was making air origami. Real smooth, Ry. At least she was laughing now.

I took a deep breath, forced my head to get screwed on straight and tried again.

"Do you know how magic connects in a mated pair?" I asked and she blushed so fast that I once again only realized too late what I had said. Well, no turning back now, which was great because Mira had noticed my blush and was already leaning in to me with her biggest grin.

"No, I don't Ryland. Wanna tell me?" The sassy girl was already turning me to jelly. I was having a hard time feeling my face, everything felt numb.

I ran my hand through my hair, jumping off the bed as I instantly began to pace.

"When I met you in the hospital way back before... ummm... everything..." Better not to go into that any more than necessary. For both our sakes. "When I first touched your hand I was supposed to test your magic, but when our magic interacted it sparked. A light bulb flickered--"

"I remember."

"It was our magic recognizing its other half. Sometimes it's small. Sometimes it's an explosion." And takes out half of the giant mansion your father built. Although with Jos, everything was different, our magic sparked in the same connection, but for a different reason.

I shook my head, not wanting to think about that now.

"Are you saying that I feel the way I do about you because of that connection?" she asked, and I actually wasn't sure how to answer without hurting her feelings. Not that I hadn't already been doing great at phrasing things poorly.

"No. Because I wasn't the biggest fan of yours for a while, even with that connection." I tried not to harden my voice, but it did anyway. "You didn't like me either, Mira."

Her jaw hardened, her eyes growing dark as she stared at me. It was the face she had every night she couldn't sleep and would come to my room. The same face as when she was working through something hard, or when that someone else's voice was loud in her head.

"Tell him to leave, Míra. This conversation is just for us." I was firm, and she nodded, her face instantly relaxing.

"I feel the way I do about you because I have grown to feel that way, not just because our magic has sparked," I said after a moment, and she stood, standing just a few feet from me as I continued to pace. "The connection of our magic just makes the feeling stronger." And makes everything more confusing. I didn't say that last part aloud, but mostly because Míra had grabbed my arm, pulling me around to face her.

She stood there, more than a foot shorter than me, this tiny girl with long blonde hair and an attitude so sassy she put Wyn to shame. But right then she was the vulnerable girl I saw at night, the strong one that put on a brave face. The capable Chosen that she only let me see sometimes.

"Míra?" I asked, my heart choking on the word.

"You said 'I feel'." Her voice was just as constricted as mine. "How do you feel, Ryland?"

Well, I had walked right into that one.

"I love you, Míra," I whispered, both of us frozen as though time had slowed. Maybe it had. Or maybe it had sped up judging by how my chest was trying to take off. "I love your hurricanes and your sweeping calms. I love the broken bits, the messy bits, and the sarcasm bits that I never know how to react to. I love all that you've overcome and while I may not love the past, I do love the future. Yes, I am older than you, and I may not act on those feelings just yet. But someday I hope you will be mine."

I was sure I was missing something, or had said something wrong, but Míra jumped up, wrapping her arms around me as she hugged me, as her cold wet nose pressed against my neck. I hadn't even realized she had been crying.

"I'll take that for now," she whispered in my ear before pulling back, a look that only spelled trouble in her eyes. "But if anyone in the Ryland fan club comes knocking, it's not my fault if they end up dead."

"Míra," I scolded, but she just giggled and skipped to her bed, grabbing the pieces of the letter before pressing them back into my hand. Her skin against mine, her magic pouring into me.

The two powerful waves connected, crashing like their own storm as they begged for more. She just smiled, even as I froze, my heart begging for her.

"Don't worry. I'll only kill the blonde ones."

20

ILYAN

THE HANDCUFFS HAD MADE A RETURN.

Although this time they were in the form of zip ties. The thin band of plastic dug into the skin of my wrists as they strapped me to the leg of the chair I sat in. They pulled me down into an awkward fold, the skin rubbed raw from the pressure.

It was the line of pressurized fire around my wrists that I felt first. A pain in my head came second as the chair shifted, rocking me to the side and slamming me into the hard metal seat in front of me. The world spun as the pain doubled, the impact from where the butt of the gun had knocked me out swelling as a new pain flowered over my skull.

Groaning as everything shifted, the world slowly began to swim into focus. The sound of wheels on a track buzzed in my ears, the signature chug-chug that I had heard for so many years when I worked on the railroad rising to meet it.

I attempted to shift my weight, but my arms held me in place as the train continued to shift and sway. Resigned to my uncomfortable fetal position, I opened my eyes to a battered train car. Ribbons of moonlight flowed over the darkness of the long space revealing lines of dilapidated chairs beside broken

REBECCA ETHINGTON

windows that worked to flood the cabin with frozen air. Everything shifted as the train jerked again, an old chandelier rocking dangerously from a single wire as a chair two rows up completely toppled over.

A groan followed the collapse, the sound out of place against the creaking of metal and wood. It was only after the sound, after the chairs began to shift against their bolts that I realized that this must be the transport that the Russian had spoken of.

Attempting to shift again, I looked from chair to chair, seeing the shadows of a few others as they flitted in and out of the dark blue light. Each occupant swayed awkwardly from their own chair, their bodies flopping dangerously from the weird positions they had been placed in. Heads rolled, mouths lolled, and each and every one of them was as unconscious as I was supposed to be.

The train shifted again, slamming my head into the heavy metal chair once again. Pops of bright white light speckled my vision as pain blossomed through my skull. The pain spread through my bones in a rattle before congregating in my joints in little tense pockets. Clenching my teeth, I kept the yelp of pain restrained, although only just.

"Hey," I hissed through the dark, my voice a slur thanks to some drug they had given me. To ensure 'safe passage', I supposed. Either that or this was just how it felt to wake up from being knocked out.

The train rocked and this time I groaned, the same word coming again, although I wasn't sure if it was said to the other unconscious passengers, or whoever was supervising. Neither responded. It was only the groan of wood and creak of metal as the train continued its journey down the tracks.

Pain swelling, I watched the light shift over the others, the blue and black making the already forgotten space look haunted. It was calming, somehow, although that sensation could have been from the injury mortality infected me with.

Either way, it made every sway of the train feel like a gentle lull...

I wasn't sure if I fell asleep or was just startled by the loud horn of the train. The angry sound bled twice through the icy air as the train began to turn, every limp body twisting to the left as everything rattled and shook. I tensed at the motion, unable to fight the pull of gravity as my body was jerked to the side.

As though it was a dance, every rag doll shifted. All but one.

A woman that I recognized at once.

"Ovailia?" The question was brimming with confusion as she scowled down at me, a million emotions hidden behind the hate in her eyes.

"Hello brother," she glowered, the sound of her voice barely audible above the sound of the train. She herself was barely visible. Dressed all in black and hidden underneath a sleek leather coat, if it wasn't for the long hair she always wore down, and the haunting blue of her eyes, I may never have seen her there.

"I didn't expect to see you here. I wonder if they know the prize they have caught." She grabbed the strands of my hair and pulled them back so I could see her. "With these buffoons I doubt it."

"What are you doing here?" I hissed through the clench in my jaw, trying to pull my head away and relieve some of the pressure from my neck, but she held on tighter, shaking me around a bit as the train shifted.

"Collecting what belongs to me."

I tensed as my head finally dropped, the heavy thing looking back to her as she drifted in and out of focus.

Her hand moved from my head to my chest, palm flat against

the tattered shirt I wore as my heart rate accelerated past what was normal or healthy.

"I will leave this for later, however. I have more important charges." She smiled at me as I looked back, only seeing the bright blue of her eyes for a second before she leaned over me, lips nestled in the hollow of my ear.

"Take care of it will you?" Her voice had changed, the tone filling with a sincerity that wrapped around us both, so many memories of growing up together traveling on its back.

Her breath was hollow in my ear as she waited for an answer, hand tightening around my shoulder as the scent of her perfume permeated the icy air. I said nothing, I couldn't. I could only watch as she kissed me on the cheek, the love I saw there fading as she stepped away.

"Ovailia," the whisper of her name never left my lips as the train continued to rock, the motions pulling her in and out of my vision like the flicker of a candle. Until, with one final rock she was gone altogether, leaving a girl with spiky black hair and a nose ring behind.

I only saw the unfamiliar girl for a moment before she too left with the rock of the train, another horn sounding as we began to turn, and my head intersected with the chair once more.

21

ILYAN

"ILYAN?"

Her soft voice pulled me out of the distorted darkness of the train car and right into the bright white beach of our Tŏuha. I knew what it was before I opened my eyes. I could hear it in the waves and the call of the birds, I could smell it in the salty air.

"Joclyn," I sighed her name as I turned to her, instinctively reaching out and pulling her into me. "Můj navždy"

The hot whisper of her breath over my neck as she burrowed into it sent shivers down my spine.

Pulling her closer, I pressed my lips against her jaw before finally opening my eyes to the intense silver grey of hers.

"Joclyn, I whispered, letting the tips of my fingers run over her face.

The sensation rippled through her and she shivered, but the look in her eyes made it clear that we both knew what was missing.

"Do you think you made the right choice?" she asked, vocalizing my fear in a way that I could not.

Fitting seeing as she was only a projection of the woman my soul longed for.

"I am not sure," I admitted, my focus shifting to the way my fingers were running over her skin, as though the more I focused the more likely it would be that I would feel her magic connect to mine.

"I still question the loss of my magic. But being here, with you, knowing what I do..." I hesitated, pressing my palm against the curve of her neck. "I couldn't find you without knowing about you. About Imdalind. About what we have been through. About this place."

She smiled, the pure joy I had seen all those years ago in the sight, and all those times since streaming out from her.

"And now?"

"And now that I have remembered you," I hesitated, leaning closer as I pulled her into me. "Now, I can find you."

For years I dreamed of her, I held her in my arms and fantasized about being with her once again. I longed to kiss her, to press my lips to hers.

I never did.

Perhaps it was the fear of the man without memories, the insecurities of not knowing who I was and what the girl before me meant to me.

Now, I knew. Now, nothing was going to stop me.

I pulled her into me as I kissed her, pressing her body against mine as I wrapped my legs around hers, winding us together.

My lips devoured hers, pressed against hers as I felt her tongue flick against my lower lip. I groaned at the touch, the soft feeling of her kiss growing into an intense pressure as she leaned against me, her arms pulling her closer.

Hands ran over skin, lips pressed against necks, and everything was a tangle of passion as I finally gained the touch that I had been longing for.

The sensation was different without the charge of our magic as it interacted, different, and yet somehow the power was still there.

I had felt my love for her before, felt the strength of my commitment and passion, but without the connection in our magic to back it up, I felt it so much more acutely.

It was just as strong as I expected it to be.

"I know this is not a true Tòuha," I whispered between the kisses that I pressed against her neck. "But this..."

"The love is real," Joclyn moaned as she shifted herself ever closer, "perhaps this is too."

As much as I wanted to believe her, I knew it was not true.

"Not yet," I gasped as I pressed my hand against her collarbone, holding her away from me just enough that I could see the silver sheen in her eyes. "But it will be soon."

She smiled at the promise, that same coy joy dancing behind her eyes. "Sounds like you have some work to do."

"I do," I whispered, letting my finger trail down the line in her jaw. "I have so much to talk to you about."

"I am sure I do too," she smiled. The game in her voice was apparent. "I hope you find me."

She smiled as she leaned closer, her eyelashes tickling against my cheek as she closed them to kiss me.

I felt her lips for the briefest moment before they were gone, gone like the sound of the waves, gone like the salt air.

And all that was left was the smell of antiseptic, a familiar rhythmic beeping undulating from somewhere in the distance.

My eyes fluttered open to the same red flowers, the same yellow light that streamed from the open window. Only this time, instead of the bitter mountain air it was crisp, cool. It reminded me of the meadowed hills in France where Wyn and Thom had made their home. If I closed my eyes I was sure I could see the tiny three-room cabin he had built. He only told me later that he had refused to use magic on the precious thing.

That memory was one of the few that mixed good with bad in a seamless wave. The emotion washed over me and I gasped, chest tensing as the intensity caught me off guard.

Much like everything else the sensation was intensified without my magic to stifle it.

Just like the pain in my head...

I turned from the window to the heavy wooden door that was inset against the yellow wallpaper. The whole room was different from the hospital I had been in Kiev, the layout was wrong, the smell that drifted in through the window didn't even match. But that wallpaper, that wallpaper was exactly the same.

I stared at it, the low hum of my heart rate monitor picking up as I attempted to sit. My movements, however, were hindered by a single padded strap wrapped around my left ankle.

Heart rate turning into a thunder, I threw the blankets from me, revealing an old stained hospital gown and one of the padded restraints that had held me down for years.

Without thinking, I pushed my magic to serge, just the same as I had always done. The concentration, the strength, it was all there, but nothing else responded.

This was going to take some getting used to.

My sigh turned into a growl as I shifted my weight, ready to tear the metal padlock on the ankle restraint off with my bare hands. I didn't get a chance to try.

The door swung open with a clatter and I jerked, throwing the blanket back over the thing.

Instead of the angry Russian, or the line of soldiers, however, it was a woman. My hope swelled as she backed her way into the room, heart thundering at her long brown hair pulled into a bun at the nape of her neck.

"Kaye!" I practically yelled her name, relief at seeing her, at seeing the one person who could possibly get me out of here.

All of the hope was dashed, however, as she turned around, revealing a nameless woman with bottle green eyes and a comfortable expression.

"Who?" she asked as she shuffled in, pulling a large metal rack behind her.

"I... ummm," I stammered, failing to come up with an adequate response.

She didn't seem to care, however, she just smiled kindly, and continued to roll her cart in, bringing it right up to where I sat up in my bed.

"It's Borscht again today." Her smile faltered somewhat, the light in her eyes dimming as though she was delivering bad news.

I felt none of that, after so long of unknowingly eating meat, a bowl of beet stew sounded divine. Unless... "Does it taste bad?"

Her smile softened, a gentle clang hitting against the side table as she set a bowl and a few rolls down on my bedside table.

"No." She didn't even look at me, her focus was only on the bowl as she carefully removed the foil. "But it has only been borscht here for a year."

Her honesty caught me off guard and I looked away from the soup that my stomach was growling in need of, to the young woman with a kindness so different from what I had seen before.

It was such a stark contrast that it made me wonder if it was all a dream.

"Where am I?" My own stomach twisted at my question.

The woman froze in her task of putting yet another roll on my tray and turned to me slowly, the trepidation I had expected to see there before flooding her once bright eyes.

"They don't want me to tell you that," she whispered, glancing at the door as she began to shift through something in the bottom of her cart.

"The Republic?" I asked part of me hoping that I could get some answers out of his woman.

She only nodded, and while it was enough, I could feel myself needing more.

"I do not have much time," she hissed, her voice shaking as the fear I had expected to see earlier presented itself. "I only bring the food... and this..."

She shoved the book toward me, the spine bulging from a pen she had concealed inside of it.

"A book?"

"They say you have no memory. But I know who you are. If you remember, even a little bit, I can help." She smiled with a pride and bravery that I would not have expected from her up until this point. "If you write letters. I will get them where they need to go."

Her hand was kind as she placed it on my arm, one gentle squeeze pressing against me before she stood.

"But the Republic..." I said, my desperation for knowledge growing as she turned to leave.

"They are not the SSU. They will not hurt you the same, although they may not be kind." Her back was to me now, her cart clattering as she pushed it toward the door. "Read the book. Fill its pages for me."

Her instructions were a hiss as the door opened, the wide wooden slab opening to swallow her whole and dispense the blonde individual that I had expected to see the first time.

I was only barely able to conceal the book underneath the covers of my bed before his focus shifted from the attractive young woman to me, his interest not wanting to leave her.

"Welcome, home, I guess we can say." His voice was a drawl, his Russian clipped in what I could only assume was agitation.

He walked right up to my bed, pulling a clipboard off the end of it as he made his way to the head. His focus drifted between me and the papers, the side glances tensing through my already taut muscles.

"A slight concussion, it seems, but other than that you appear to have come through transport okay."

He sighed and set the clipboard down on the bed, right on top of where I had placed the book. I was shocked he hadn't noticed that it hadn't hit the bed.

"I suppose now the only matter at hand is the question of whether or not you will comply, or if we will have to resort to other tactics."

I swallowed. The strict consonants in his words made it clear just how serious he was, and that promise of torture did not bode well for me and my suddenly mortal existence.

"What exactly do you want to know?"

He smiled at the fear that, like it or not, was quickly taking up residence in my heart.

I was sure I could battle him. I was sure I could win. It was only one restraint on my ankle, one man, with one gun. But even with my memory of how to fight returned, there was little to nothing I could do.

It wasn't worth the risk.

He stepped forward, pulling a few pieces of paper from the back of the clipboard and placed them down on the bed.

I had seen the pictures so often in the years I spent in the fog of not knowing. They were the same ones of the battle in Svarov, of Prague being rebuilt, and that last one with Joclyn and Ryland walking along the bank of the Vltava River, Joclyn refusing to take the long golden ribbon from him.

My heart clenched at seeing it there, at seeing her hair flow free around her face and not bound in the braid. It was a pain of loss I finally understood, the same look clear on her face as she pleaded with my brother to take the sacred ribbon. I saw it in her, just as I felt it in myself now.

Even though I knew the risk, knew that the man beside me was watching me intently, I still grabbed the picture from the pile, warm tears rolling down my cheeks.

"Ahhh," The man sighed, the tone of his voice sounding as though he had found a great treasure. "You know her then?"

The picture was wrinkled, worn around the edges, with a bit of both water and fire damage to the delicate print. They all were. I dropped the treasured picture of my wife and shifted to another one, the exact one Kaye had used to help identify Joclyn all those years before.

She and I, fighting side by side.

The pain of the other image was gone here, although I could barely see it thanks to the damage that the images had received.

"Is this the same girl?" I asked, careful to keep my voice casual.

"The same..." He obviously didn't understand.

"The same girl in the image?" I asked, a thought slamming into me, making my heart rate monitor beat faster in my excitement. The man obviously didn't notice. "Is she the same? I cannot see her here. Do you have the original."

I looked right at him as I asked the question, watched his breath catch as he went back to the clipboard, shuffling through papers as he tried to locate something.

"You were shown these images before," he finally said, his voice gaining that same hard line of lost patience. "You do not need an original. You know what you see."

He glared at me, fingers tapping on the clipboard in either impatience or nerves, I wasn't sure. The sound matched my heart rate as it too began to accelerate, thundering in exhilaration.

He knew nothing about me. The SSU had taken it all.

"Yes, it is the same girl," I finally said, not looking a millimeter away as I handed the images back. "But I do not know who she is."

He stared at me, the corners of his jaw tensing as his temper flared.

"Fine," he said in a grumble so low that I wasn't completely sure that was what he had said. "Then tell me about this."

This picture was different. The image was clean, crisp, with no sign of damage.

It was clearly of me flying over the town at the border, moments away from escape.

I could see Kaye and the others below me, see their fear. I knew this moment, just seeing it pricked me with the memory of dozens of bullets ripping through my body.

This time I was the one to hesitate, although I did not look away. I refused to give this man all of my strength, I could still feel the twist of fear in my stomach that the memory of those years of torture had left me with.

"Whatever power was in me. Whatever power this man had," I said as I tapped against my own image. "It was lost in that escape. I have told you before. It is gone...."

"No." His snap was not in anger, but instead in a defiant command of refusal. He would not believe me, or rather he would not fail in bringing this power to his precious Republic.

I could only imagine the accolades that would be behind it.

"You spout lies so you can escape in the night," he hissed in Russian, some of the papers in his hands slipping to the ground as he leaned closer to me. "You think I will believe you, but you are my prisoner and I know better. I will not believe you."

The rest of the clipboard fell to the ground with a clang that made me jump, the action so abrupt that even if I had been paying attention I don't think I could have moved fast enough to stop him from slicing the long blade over my arm.

I screamed as the flesh opened, as my own blood began to pour from me in a wave brighter and faster than I had ever seen.

I had never felt pain as strong as I did then. Never felt every moment of a cut, or an injury.

I had been hurt thousands of times. My bones had been broken, even injuries worse than this had ripped over me. Before, however, I always had my magic to soothe the pain, to heal me. Now, there was none of that. Now, there was no barrier between me and the pain.

I continued to scream as the sheets of the bed blossomed in red from the pool that was pouring over my skin. The Russian held my arm down as he stared at the massive gash, waiting in exhilaration for a forgotten magic to erupt in me. Nothing happened.

"It's gone," I panted through the agony, wishing beyond anything that it was here.

That the pain would leave.

"The magic is gone." I barely got the words out before I fell back on the bed, unable to support my own weight through the lightheaded spin I was smothered by.

"No!" I heard his scream as my hand dropped, as his feet stomped, as the door slammed shut.

I heard it, but I could only look at the stained ceiling, at the old hospital light, and wish beyond anything that I could escape this place.

That I could Stutter and find myself in the safety of her arms.

But there was nothing but an old ceiling, a tight restraint, and the hard edge of a book against my lower back.

The book.

The woman with the kind face who promised to help me. Told me to write letters to them. To find help.

It was a long shot, and I wasn't sure how I could make it work, how I could find Joclyn, but I had to try.

Just like Kaye, I had to trust her.

22

JOCLYN

"Any update?" I asked as Ryland entered the room, Míra only steps behind him. The girl had a look on her face that was both smug and awed. Clearly she wasn't going to be leaving Ryland's side anytime soon.

Ryland shook his head no. "The final team got back from scouring Mongolia just a few minutes ago. Nothing. My guess is the place is cloaked."

"Or it's so small you can't see it with the naked eye," Wyn added.

"Or it's underground," Thom said, leaning back in his chair.

"Or he's not there," I whispered, biting my lower lip. That one was the most probable given what I had seen in my sight. Nastya torturing Ilyan, Ivory making machines, explosions, the tip of a needle smothered in clouds, prayer flags strung through a forest. It was the prayer flags I had seen the most, lines and lines of them weaved through a forest as though they were leading me to something.

I closed my eyes, exhaling sharply as I ran back through the sight, the same words as before buzzing in my head.

"*In the high mountains. Far from the plains. In the islands, against the land. Find them marching. Defeat the fire. Take the source. Repair the land."* The words rumbled in my head, but I kept them there. The more I tried to figure it out, the less it made sense. That was usual for sight, but this time it was even more frustrating.

In the mountains, but an island against the land...

"Japan." I shook my head again. "Maybe we were right originally and he's in Japan. It fits better with the mountains and the island being close to the land. Besides, we know the Kyō are there."

I was mostly talking to myself. I was sure everyone else would think I was talking gibberish, but thankfully none of them looked at me like I had lost it. They were probably all too used to me doing that at this point. Well, all but Míra, but I wasn't even sure she was aware of the world around her. She was still looking all twitterpated from where she leaned against the wall, staring at the back of Ryland's head.

The room we were in was the one we always used for meetings, the stone was still rough and pockmarked from the war, but the wooden table was large enough for all of us. Wyn had even tried to make it a circle at one point.

For now, Wyn, Thom, Ryland, and I all sat in a weird array of whatever chairs we had been able to scavenge, the table between us. Normally, the rough wood surface was stacked with maps or reports or whatever else we needed. Today it was bare. Something which Rinax had already pointed out twice from where he perched on the high back of Ryland's chair.

"I thought your sight said Mongolia?" Wyn asked after a minute, her holey hand flat against the table.

"Technically, my sight didn't say anything." I shrugged, letting my finger run over the surface of the table. "But the terrain looked like Mongolia. I haven't been to Japan enough to know, so I guess it could be the same."

"To be honest, I don't think we could get everyone to agree to start the fight in the middle of nowhere Mongolia, anyway." Thom's chair scraped against the ground as he stood, going over to the only other piece of furniture in the room, the cabinet with all the maps.

"All of the Chosen's lives are in danger," Thom continued as he began to thumb through the stacks of paper, pulling out one and then another. "Now that the SSU has fallen, the caves of Imdalind are the only safe place to be. And you all know as well as I do that we won't be able to bring all the Chosen here. Some won't make it, more will be created. Hell, we don't even know where they all are. The Kyō will get them."

"So the SSU is defeated then?" Míra asked, pushing herself off the wall as she stepped toward the table. She shrunk back against the wall the second I looked up at her.

This was the first time she had been allowed in this room, and she clearly wasn't going to miss out on this chance.

"Well, seeing as you beheaded their leader, yes, I would say they have fallen," I said, the girl grinning even as Wyn looked like she was about to heave over the side of the table.

"Looks like I trained you well," Wyn said confidently, even if she did look a little green. The compliment, however, sent Míra beaming more.

"Yeah, let's just not make a habit of it, kay?" Ryland was clearly trying to hide a smile, his eyes all bright and moonstruck as he looked at her.

"Anyway," Thom barked, slamming the maps he had retrieved from the cabinet onto the table. "The last of the colonies got here about an hour before you all got back. They are ready for war, and they are ready for it now."

Thom unfurled the map of Japan first, his finger already pressed into the center, just off from Tokyo.

"The Kyō are here, The Tokyo Sky Tree, not that they hid it,"

Thom tapped the map a few times before sitting back down again. "It was only a few hours after they conducted their not-so-hostile takeovers that they declared it the new capital. That's where our people want to go. And I don't think there's any way to stop them."

Thom shook his head, dreads swinging as he sat back in his chair and looked right at me.

"We had to stop two groups from leaving while you guys were gone. If we want to go together, and have a chance of catching them off guard, we need to go soon." Wyn gave Thom a look before turning back to me. That same look of regret everyone had given me over the last few hours catching me in my chest again.

"What are the chances of Ilyan being in Tokyo?" Ryland asked, his hand halfway to the map when Rinax landed in the center of it, his little face pulled into a scowl as he stared Ryland down. I would have laughed, but before I could even inhale that frightening face was turned toward me.

How could something that was essentially a giant blue glitter fairy be so terrifying?

"What is it Rinax?" I tried to keep my voice level, but the guy was freaking me out.

"You two, have got to look at the bigger picture." His high pitched voice was near a snarl as he continued to look between us. "You have a world who is now capturing the Chosen and you are moaning about your husband! I left three years ago and you were pouting about your husband. I come back, and you are still pouting about your husband. It's pathetic! You need to focus on saving your people and not spend years crying about someone that you've already been told you'll get back."

"You have no idea what you are talking about!" I snapped, jumping to my feet as I leaned over the table to stare down the little monster. "You left days after my husband, my mate, vanished! You come back days after we figure out where he is. Don't think that your disappearance and bad timing are a worthy sample of everything else that's been happening here. We've been saving the Chosen. We've been capturing your people even though they want to rip our faces off, just like you threw a fit about all those years ago. Don't come back and pretend to be some vigilante ready to save our asses. You left to go find your family. I didn't see you trying to help us save the world. Now that it's time for me to find my family, you don't get a say."

I was ragey, and I knew it. I had been since I watched Míra cut off the head of the one person that would know where Ilyan was. The one person who had actually seen him. It boiled over the edge when *Ivory* spouted out all she had done to him. Rinax was just getting the full brunt of it.

To be honest, though, he kinda deserved it. More so seeing as he just scowled at me with that pug nose of his. Arrogant glitter monster.

"I can do both, Rinax. I can save my mate and I can save the world. If I can do it in one shot, I will. Don't think for a second that I have forgotten what I am and what my role is." I was sure my eyes had gone black with how everyone was staring at me as I sat back down.

Well, everyone but Wyn who was grinning and giving me a silent applause from where she sat behind Rinax. It was probably good he didn't see her and her overexaggerated applause, he was just as pissed as I was.

"Now, who is ready to kick some ass, save the world, and find our king?" I was well aware I was in full queen mode. I didn't need the matching smug grins from Thom and Ryland to tell me that. Hell, even Míra was looking at me like she was about to bow down and sing my praises.

"We have about five thousand Chosen who are trained

enough I feel comfortable sending them in to fight. There are three hundred Skřítek who can lead them," Thom said, tapping on the map and letting pin pricks of color appear there as he organized the army.

"Don't forget one Drak," I added, tapping the map to contribute my own mark.

"This Vilý is out," Rinax said, still snarling. I resisted the urge to roll my eyes. Of course after his little speech he would bail on us.

"So is this Trpaslík." Wyn's voice was so quiet that I almost didn't even recognize it was her. She sat, looking a bit grumpy at her announcement, even as Thom smiled and grabbed her hand.

Everything about that was just melting me, and not just because I knew why. I nodded in understanding and removed a few dots from the board all while doing my best not to smile too big.

Being a stoic, powerful Queen was hard sometimes.

"What?" Ryland asked, practically jumping up in confusion. "Since when do you say no to going in and burning things to the ground?"

"Since I went ahead and decided to grow a demon in my uterus, Ryland," Wyn prodded him in a mock voice. Well, I hadn't expected her to announce it that way.

Neither had Thom considering he dropped his head in his hands.

"What?" Ryland asked in confusion. He was either really slow or needed to go back to eighth grade biology.

Míra however was squealing and bouncing around behind him. Even Rinax looked excited. I had never seen him smile before, like really smile. It was creepy as hell. His face was all distorted, the sharp points of his teeth visible as his eyes seemed to gleam. He looked like he was about to eat the baby, not celebrate it.

"This was really not how I wanted to tell my brother, Wyn," Thom moaned from behind his hands. "We talked about this."

"Yes, and I didn't think it would be so hard to say no to going into battle. It just kinda slipped out."

"Some slip," I giggled, at least I could tell everyone now. I was so excited for them and keeping it a secret for even as little time as I had was nearly impossible.

"Can someone please help a guy out?" Ryland asked. Kay, maybe he was that stupid.

"I'm knocked up, Ry." Somehow that made more sense to Ryland.

His eyes got wide, a smile spreading over his face as he danced around the table and gathered both of them up in his arms.

I was halfway around the table to join in the hug dance when the door opened, and one of the guards that I knew had been assigned to the survivors from the SSU attack slipped in. My magic sparked, every warning alarm going off as I turned to him.

"Kirl?" I asked, everything going on high alert as the squealing, giggling mosh pit silenced, even though they didn't let go over each other.

"I'm so sorry to bother you, it's just that..." He glanced around the room before opening the door further, revealing a haggard old woman I had never seen before. Her nurse's uniform was torn and stained, her brown and grey streaked hair had mostly pulled free from a bun that was covered in dirt. She looked scared, something that faded away as she looked up to me.

"She claims to know Ilyan."

"What do you mean she know--" I began.

"I know you!" Míra cut me off, rushing from where she stood against the back wall of the room to face the old woman. She looked up at Míra's call, recognition lighting her features. "You're Katenka! This is the nurse from the hospital in Kiev!"

"I was also the nurse to your husband for three years," she said with a nod to Míra before she looked right back at me. "He's been looking for you."

23

JOCLYN

THE WORLD FELT NUMB.

Everything felt numb. I sat between Ryland and Wyn, their hands wrapped around my own as I listened to everything Katenka had to say. Listened to what had happened the last three years this woman and her daughter, Kaye, had cared for my husband.

How he didn't remember anything. How he pieced together dreams to try to find me. How Nastya used him.

I knew part of me should be sad. I was sure Wyn and Ryland expected me to be with how they sat on either side of me. But I was just pissed, and I was getting angrier by the second.

"So, Nastya spent years torturing him, seeing how far she could push his magic?" I asked, my voice strained thanks to the tightness in my jaw. Katenka nodded.

"Míra?" I asked as I stood, dropping Ry and Wyn's hands as I turned to her. The girl's eyes widened as she jumped to attention. She actually looked scared.

"Yes?"

"Thank you for cutting that woman's head off." I gave her a hug, Míra stiff and lost beneath me as Ryland chuckled. I would have to assume that the gasp and 'my stars' that echoed from the door in Ukrainian came from Katenka.

"And thank you for helping me." I turned back to Katenka who was still looking lost in the doorway. I held out my hand, but she just stared at it. "Thank you for caring for my husband."

She didn't move for a minute, she just stared at my hand, almost as though she was scared of it.

"They say you're the Queen, is that true?" she asked in nearly a whisper, looking back at me with wide eyes. Her trepidation suddenly made sense. I nodded. "So, Ja- Ilyan... he really was a King?"

I paused, I had spent the last few minutes listening to what she had to say about Ilyan. But we hadn't told her anything about him.

"Is a King," I corrected, "and, yes." I grinned, and waved Thom over from where he had been lounging in his chair, making origami dinosaurs out of the maps. "This is his brother, Thom, and his other brother Ryland. Ilyan has been the king for--" I had to stop, my brain going on overdrive as I rubbed my nose. "I don't actually know."

Thank god for Wyn. She laughed jumping to her feet as she threw her arm around my shoulders.

"Don't worry. I got this. I'm the oldest one here save for the winged sourpuss." She knocked her head back, Katenka's eyes following to the winged Vilỳ who was neither brown nor poisoned. Her eyes widened into saucers so big that I actually tried to get Wyn to stop. All of this information had come as a shock to me, I had no clue how Katenka was going to take it. Just seeing Rinax appeared to be pushing her over the edge.

"Ilyan was born like a thousand years ago, started ruling about two hundred years after that. He's old." Thankfully Wyn seemed to see what I did and reeled her explanation in, keeping it short, before poor Katenka exploded from shock.

"He's also very powerful. If Nastya truly knew what she had-
-" I pressed my lips together, not wanting to think about it
anymore. "I need to find him. Save him." My voice choked as my
heart seized in my chest and I turned back to the maps that held
a million possibilities of where Ilyan could be.

They were also folded into giant paper dinosaurs.

"I think I can help with that, too." I turned back to Katenka
so fast I was pretty sure I smacked Ryland in the face with my
hair.

"You can?"

She nodded, "My daughter, Kaye, she's quite the whizz with
stuff like that. She has a tracker on the dark web. I know the
code to the site. I just need a phone."

Before she had finished speaking three phones were
extended to her, all of them blazing to life thanks to our magic.

She looked at them before grabbing the one closest to her
and typing a few things into a browser.

"This is the only thing I know how to do on these. She
taught me, just in case we could ever get out..." A few more taps
and she turned the phone to me, to a map of the globe and the
three dots that were flashing. One for Kaye, one for Katenka,
and one in the middle of Mongolia.

"Ilyan," I gasped, reaching out to the light as though I would
be able to just pull him through the phone.

He was right there. I was right.

I snatched the phone before anyone could stop me, using my
two fingers to zoom in as much as I could. I could barely see the
building on the satellite images from the phone. No wonder the
scouts hadn't seen anything.

The building was a wide mass, clearly painted and designed
to blend in with the landscape. There were even trees growing in
between the narrow wings, so if you weren't paying attention
you would just think it was another building.

Except it was a building that housed the most precious thing in the word.

Well, to me anyway.

Phone in hand, I raced back to the table and to the maps that Thom had thankfully unfolded. China, Mongolia, and Japan were spread over the table top. My fingers were already stretching out.

"Here," I said, marking the map with my magic. Looking at the spot on the map and the detail on the phone in turn. "This tracker is clear enough that I bet I could Stutter in and get him. I mean, he's right there..."

Again, I resisted the urge to fondle the blinking dot on the phone.

"How did she do that?" Ryland asked, looking over my shoulder to the phone. "Most of the towers are down. We can only get our phones to work because of our magic."

Katenka just shrugged. "I have no clue with that girl. I don't even know what she's using to track me. She didn't tell me about it until a few days ago. I wasn't too happy to learn she's put something *inside me.*"

Katenka shuddered in horror, but I rushed her, wrapping my arms around her.

"I take it this helps?"

"It does." I gave her another squeeze before I turned to everyone, only vaguely aware that Katenka was sneaking out the door. "Who is ready to finish this?"

Once again, everyone raised their hands, everyone but Wyn who was looking quite grumpy about it. Even Míra had raised her hand, which earned her a look from both Ryland and me.

"If Wyn's not coming you are going to need me. Besides, I'm pretty sure I proved myself." And the smug grin was back. I hated that she was right.

I also hated that everyone in this room knew if we didn't

bring her she would just follow us anyway. Considering how pale Ryland had just gone, I was thinking I needed to find a place where she could do some damage and still be safe.

"Fine. But no more cutting off heads, and you stick to Thom's side like glue." I was firm. Both she and Thom did not seem too happy about my decision.

"You can't be serious?" Thom was nearly whining.

"Why can't I stick with Ryland?" So was Míra.

"Ryland is with me," I said, cutting them both off. Rinax sat up from where he had been lounging in a chair but I gave him a warning glare. I didn't want to deal with his sourpuss expression right now.

"Ry and I are going to get Ilyan," I tapped on the map of China where Ilyan was, "Thom, you and Míra are going to lead the armies right to the Kyō headquarters."

"Wait. All of them?" Thom was looking at the mark of the Kyō headquarters in the middle of Japan's map in confusion, I just smiled.

"All of them. They will be so focused on the masses heading their way they won't even notice Ry and I coming. We'll get Ilyan--"

"And if the leader of the Kyō is there I'll find him." Ryland was firm, maybe even beaming. "Worst case we get Ilyan out and then meet up with you. We are finishing this today."

This was it, we had found Ilyan, we knew where the Kyō were, we had an army ready to fight, and a foolproof way to get there.

"And I will be Queen Empress," Wyn said, rising to her feet as though she was already taking the crown.

"Wouldn't you have to be at the battle to take the throne?" Míra asked through a giggle. Wyn turned on her, eyes flashing dangerously as the true Queen Empress she would be shone through.

"A good Queen Empress knows when to strike. Besides, unless vomit turns into a good weapon, you don't want me on this trip."

"Ew." Míra was officially no longer gushing over the baby.

"Okay, when do we leave?" Ryland pulled us all back as he straightened the maps.

I put my hands over his, knowing he was going to hate what I was going to say next.

"How about now?"

"Oh, no," Ryland moaned. Wyn suddenly wasn't the only one who had gone green.

"How quick can you get the army moving, Thom?" I didn't look away from Ryland. I needed him to know how serious I was.

"With how antsy they are, we could be in Tokyo in about thirty minutes."

"Just enough time for us to find Ilyan." I stood, holding my hand out to Ryland who, as pale as he was, actually looked determined.

"Ready?" I asked, my entire body feeling as though it was going to burst out of its skin.

Ryland looked at me, not a drop of fear in his eyes as he stepped closer and put his hand in mine.

"Let's go save my brother."

My magic surged around us as we stood there, Thom and Wyn already running to the door as Míra stared at us.

It was too late to warn her not to follow, though, we were already being pulled into the Stutter, dragged through all those ribbons of time and life as I focused on that spot on the map. Focused on that building in the middle of the mountains where Ilyan was.

When we emerged, it wasn't to him however, although judging by our surroundings we were in the right place.

The building was old, made up of dark stone and fogged glass, and full of Kyō soldiers. A hundred eyes turned to us at the pop of our arrival, eyes widening as one after another they recognized who we were.

"Okay, so maybe we should have planned this out better," Ryland sighed, already moving to stand before me.

I let my magic flare, pushing through each of the soldiers and then through the rooms of the building as I searched for him. Just like in the hospital in Kiev there was no sign of his magic. Except, this time, I knew he was here.

My magic laid out the building for me perfectly, every inch of the place mapped out as I thought back to Kaye's map and the light that was right above us.

"What would a rescue mission be without a little fun?" I quipped, grabbing Ryland's hand as I winked at him, and pulled him back into the Stutter, to a room a few floors above us, and away from the charging army.

24

ILYAN

THERE WAS ONLY one time a day the light from the window stretched far enough to reach my bed, to fall over my face and arms. I lay still, eyes closed as I attempted to transport myself to that beach. To our Tóuha.

I would get back there. Soon.

I sent more than a dozen letters, a dozen notes, with the girl. One of them would get me out of here.

I knew it would.

The warmth began to leave and I opened my eyes, stretching my hands toward the beam of sun that fell over the edge of the bed. The light made weird shadows over my skin as the curtains billowed in the slightly rancid air from the heater. Light and dark swirls danced over skin as the light began to fade, the warmth leaving along with it.

Still, I did not move.

The creak of the door sounded behind me, the sound of rusty hinges a soft whisper before gentle feet stepped into the room, each step hesitant. I didn't even turn, I just lay still, staring at the window.

Had I paid attention to the steps, I would have recognized his approach. I would have recognized the tap of his leather shoes. I would have expected to see the blond crop of his hair and the dead pierce of his eyes.

I would have braced for it.

But now, the appearance of the Russian filled me with a sickly combination of stubborn defiance and dread.

He stood beside my bed. His hands behind his back as he rocked on his heels, his smile growing.

The look he gave me turned me to ice, but not as much as the two words that followed.

"Ilyan Krul," he said, the slime in each syllable turning the little secret that I had hidden so well into noxious fumes that billowed in the air.

"What do you want?" I did not know how he had discovered me, or if the woman with the books had simply ratted me out, but it didn't matter. Not with the way he was looking at me.

If I was going to find a way out of here, now was the time. Magic or not, I couldn't wait any longer.

"I want what everyone else wants," he sneered, the triumph in his voice making my stomach turn. "I want the woman from Prague. I want the Oheň."

I hesitated, watching him as the exhilaration of a hunted prize colored his eyes, the look becoming that much more frightening as the daylight continued to dim, the sun painting the windows in a red hue as it set.

"I do not know where she is." It was the first honest thing I had said to him, and I couldn't be more happy with the truth behind them.

He rocked on his heels, his shoulders shifting as his hands did, the motion making it clear he was hiding something behind his back. Shackles creaked as I shifted, my hands balling into hard rocks against an equally hard mattress as I prepared for the emotional and physical blows that were inevitably coming.

"Do you really think it is wise to lie to me?" he asked, the hostility in his eyes tensing my muscles further.

"I'm not..."

"I already know you are looking for your mate." The way he said the word made my stomach turn. "This... Joclyn is it? Such a pretty name for such a pretty girl."

"You..."

"Ah-ah," he stopped me, his features shifting to condescending mockery as he stepped closer to me. "You already gave me the keys to find her. To find you..."

"How?" I growled, the word barely a question. I already knew, after all.

I already knew.

Clenching my teeth as tight as I could, I kept my temper at bay, something that was proving to be much easier without the flood of magic behind it.

His smile grew as the paper he had been hiding behind his back was thrown at me. I recognized it at once, the letter I had written to a journalist in Paris, near one of the many tunnel openings and close to a safe house Wyn had used for centuries.

It had instructions on how to find the house, and written in tiny Czech at the bottom was a letter to Joclyn.

I love you, my darling. Never forget.

"You led me right to her, you know. To this little house in Paris. The place was empty. Forgotten. But now we know. Now we will find her."

Shackles clattered as I jerked toward him, ready to rip him limb from limb. My hands reached in vain, my thoughts pulling toward my nonexistent magic as I flailed in a desperate need to reach him. To hurt him.

Anything to protect her.

Unfortunately, all I had was words, "If you even get near her…"

"You will lunge through the air?" he interrupted me. He laughed at his own joke, the cold cruel sound cutting through the air like ice.

"Accept it, Ilyan," he said, the use of my real name twisting through my gut. "You can't reach me. You can't even escape that bed. If you had any of the power these pictures show you would have done it already, you would have murdered me."

He leaned in close, driving his point home, like an iron barb right into my heart. I refused to move, refused to shimmy away from his proximity. I would not give him that, no matter how true his words might be, I would not back down.

"You have nothing," he said with a sneer, his yellowed teeth far too close for comfort. "And neither does she."

"You are wrong," I said, the strength in my voice catching me off guard. I could almost feel my magic spark inside of me at the strength. "I will do nothing. I do not need to. She, however, will destroy you."

His smile faltered as the humor was wiped from his face. As much as he tried to keep it there it continued to slide away, his own fear replacing it with each word I spoke.

"You have seen the photos. You have heard the stories. You may think you know what she is capable of, but you don't. Not really. She can walk in here, stop every bullet, kill every man…"

"Does she stop bullets as well as you did during your ill-fated escape?" The question was a chuckle, but I plowed right on, refusing to let him take control of the conversation.

Refusing to let him deflate me.

"And destroy you in less time than it would take you to blink."

He blinked.

The exaggerated motion was a clear mockery of everything

that I had said. Perhaps it was. She was not here after all, she was not on her way to save me.

As much as I knew she could destroy them if she found them, and would in her attempt to reach me, I also did not know if they had been successful in finding her. I did not know the world outside of these walls.

The only consolation was that the Republic did not have all of the information. They did not know the outcome of Nastya's testing. If they did, I did not know if Joclyn would be able to combat that.

"I would like to see that." He said with a smile, the drip of warning that seeped from his voice making me shiver.

"Then keep looking for her," I said, letting my confidence bubble to the surface as I sat up straighter, the restraints around my ankles pulling awkwardly as I attempted to posture him.

"You can rest assured we will." He smiled and stepped back, pulling the clipboard from the hook on the wall, looking very much like your everyday doctor.

"Then lie in confidence of your impending death." The words were strong, the warning clear.

He stood facing me, jaw tight, before a tiny pop filled the room, the shrill sound bursting against eardrums as two people materialized between the foot of my bed and the heavily guarded door.

I stared at them, not believing what I was seeing as both my wife and my brother appeared before me in a mass of dark hair and swirling magic.

The Russian was not even able to gasp in surprise before he fell to the ground, crumpling in a heap that was heard not seen.

I could not see it, for I was only looking at her.

"Mi Lasko," I gasped as I tried to shift my weight, as I tried to shift toward her.

I had never felt so trapped.

"Ilyan!" Her voice was a wave of power, the strength crippling me with a million emotions.

Her arms wrapped around me as she lunged into my arms, head burrowing into my neck as her hair billowed around me.

She felt the same as my dreams.

She smelled the same as my dreams.

She was the same. Except this wasn't a dream. This was real.

"Joclyn," I whispered into her hair, my heart swelling as I turned into her, to the familiar smell of roses and smoke, and pressed my lips against her for the first time in years.

Her skin was hot, it burned against me, but the spark was gone, the connection was gone.

My magic was gone.

I wasn't the only one to notice it.

She turned toward me, pulling away just enough to look at me, her hands cupping the sandpaper growth on my chin. She looked at me intently, the look in her eyes making it clear she was attempting to speak into me, right into my mind, as we had before. But there was nothing, nothing but the intense gaze of her silver eyes, nothing but the pool of tears.

"It will be okay," I whispered, trying to ease the fear that had quickly taken over her. "It will be okay."

I didn't know how to fix it, I didn't know how to return the magic as I had been told I could. But, as Ryland's anxious hissing near the door was pointing out, now wasn't the time to figure it out.

"They are headed right for us," he gasped, a wall of yellow bursting from his hand as he shielded the door. "We need to go now."

The powerful man before me was so different from the scared and broken boy I had last seen.

Staring at him, at Joclyn, as she too prepared to fight, made me realize just how much time had passed, how much had changed.

How much they had grown.

There was an ache that ran through me, pushing against my heart in a longing for the lost time, for the disconnect that was threatening. The emotion was only there for a moment, the passion stronger as it filled me with a pride, with a connection to both of them.

"Ilyan's magic..." Joclyn whispered, her intense stare igniting my soul before she turned toward Ryland. "His magic is gone."

"Causing problems already, brother?" he asked with a smile, his focus clearly on the footsteps that had begun to pound through the hall, his fingertips sparking in eager anticipation.

"No problems here," I sighed, throwing the blankets back, "but I might need a little help."

Joclyn turned back to me, eyebrows arched in confusion before she looked down to my spindly legs and the massive bands that held me down. The determination for battle faded from her face, leaving a horrified 'oh' that made it clear she was ready to kill someone and not just the man who remained crumpled on the floor.

"What have they done to you?" Her voice was a growl of anger as her grip against me increased, her anger flaring much the same way mine had years before.

With a shock, I realized why.

The imposter had told me that my magic was still alive, that it was living inside of my mate, and looking at her now, I could see it.

I could see my power, but I could also see her own. It was amazing. It was -

"Beautiful," I said aloud in Czech, the one word sparking across her face in a wide smile.

"I could say the same to you," she quipped in my native

tongue, the language a beautiful song when whispered from her lips. The use of it caught me off guard, she hadn't even begun to master it all those years before.

Now it was perfected.

"Will you two stop flirting and get out of here!" Ryland suddenly yelled as the door shook, the heavy thud echoing through the momentary calm as the soldiers worked to bring down the door.

Joclyn turned from me in a fan of hair and power, jumping from the bed as she flexed her hand once toward the shivering wood. Screams filtered from the hall as her magic sent soldiers to their knees, although in death or injury I had no way of knowing.

"If you think I am leaving you alone here, Ry, you are terribly mistaken. You can't take them alone," Jos snapped at my brother, he just rolled his eyes.

"She will be here any minute, Joclyn," Ryland interrupted her, the confusing conversation sending my focus back and forth. "You can't expect her not to have followed."

Their voices roared above the increasing threats of battle that came from the other side of the door. Shouts, yells, and the heavy thuds against wood joined together into a cacophony that drowned out everything.

The sound was making me anxious, but not in the way you would expect. I was anxious to fight, anxious to destroy those who had hurt me. Mostly, however, I was anxious to get out of here, find someplace quiet and just hold Joclyn against me.

"Who are we talking about?" I yelled above the noise, the bickering friends turning toward me with differing levels of frustration on their faces. I don't think they heard me.

"She will be here," Ryland said, not looking at me as he continued to plow on, his voice rising above the sound of the now splintering wood. "You need to go."

"Bu…"

"Don't fight me Joclyn," Ryland roared, the level of his voice even silencing the army outside. "You can always come back. But if he has no magic…"

Joclyn's lips were a tight line as she turned back toward me, her hand held out in the same offer as before.

"What will happen to you if we stutter?" She asked, her voice soft as she stepped closer. Her arms were strong as she helped me to stand, although my frame was much lankier than hers.

"I do not know," I answered as honestly as I could. Although I knew it was nothing good, I was desperate enough to leave that I was willing to try.

Judging by the glimmer in Joclyn's eyes, however, she saw right through it.

"Then we will fly," she whispered, wrapping her arms around me as her powerful magic lifted us both off the ground, leaving us to hover in nothing. "And this time I will carry you."

Her smile was kind, loving, and it was that I looked at as the world shattered.

The window shattered as Ryland's magic exploded, the door flying to pieces around us as an army streamed in one way, and a woman with long blonde hair soared through the other.

For a moment I could have sworn it was Ovailia, my sister had haunted me enough over the past few years, but she was younger, far more punk rock than enchantress.

"You are in so much trouble," she yelled to nobody in particular, as she began to fight by Ryland's side. The man only laughed as he easily felled five of the heavily armed men.

"How can I protect you if you keep leaving me behind?" the new arrival yelled as she continued to fight.

"How can I protect you if you keep following me when I tell you to stay?" Ryland countered, although he was clearly trying to hide a smile. "Just shut up and kill the Republic scum."

"Fine."

"Hold on tight," Joclyn whispered as we began to move, her magic flooding me as my body disappeared and, absorbed by her magic, we soared through the air and away from the hell that had been my life for so long, and right into the dream that I had longed for.

25

RYLAND

HE WAS THERE, my brother was right there.

His hair was shorter than I had ever seen it, that alone made him look like a shadow of himself. Although, the dark circles under his eyes weren't helping. He looked as though he had been punched, starved, and was one good fall away from death.

But he was there, after so many years of looking, we had found him.

Of course, if we didn't move fast we were also going to lose him.

The army that we had originally stuttered into was already headed this way. They had recognized us, and it didn't take a rocket scientist to figure out why we were here.

"You need to go," I said as the floor began to rattle. Not many of the soldiers that were stampeding to us had magic, but I could still feel them approach like they were some kind of swarm of rats.

"Bu--"

"Don't fight me Joclyn." I gave her a look from where I stood by the door, she was still helping a very frail Ilyan to his feet. He wasn't going to be able to fight let alone get himself out of here.

Joclyn needed to focus on him. I had gotten myself out of worse. "You can always come back. But if he has no magic..."

Whatever I had been about to say faded off as the pounding on the floor grew closer. They were here.

"What will happen to you if we Stutter?" Jos mumbled to him from behind me.

Their voices were drowned by the yells of the soldiers as they beat against the wall of fogged glass that made up the entire north side of the room.

Whoever had designed this room had clearly thought ahead on how to easily stop anyone from trying to take their 'God'. One smack from the butt of a gun against the glass and it was already cracking.

Odd, with all their knowledge of a God, however, they hadn't really planned *that* far ahead. It wouldn't be that hard to keep the glass intact after all. I let my magic stretch as Joclyn lifted Ilyan, pushing the barrier against the glass in a shield even as something began to blink on the other side.

Shit. A bomb. Probably one of those lightning ones too. Okay, they *had* planned ahead.

"Get out--!" I turned, yelling to them just as the bomb on the other side of the glass exploded and shards went everywhere. Not just from the glass wall in front of me, but from the window behind.

The army may have broken through the wall of windows on one side, but a very angry Mira charged her way in through the other.

"You are in so much trouble," she snapped as she flew right to me, already flaring her magic toward the dozens of angry soldiers that had broken through. "How can I protect you if you keep leaving me behind?"

"How can I protect you if you keep following me when I tell you to stay?" I countered? My anger was flaring, even if I was happy to see her. She was grinning at me as she waved her hand and took down two of the soldiers with one spark of her magic.

"Just shut up and kill the Republic scum." I would have to handle this later. Again.

"Fine."

"Hold on tight," Joclyn yelled from behind us as she carried Ilyan through the now shattered window, her magic wrapping around them and vanishing them from sight.

Ilyan was safe. I should be rejoicing, but now Míra and I were here, facing a wall of soldiers as they streamed in toward us.

"Let's have some fun!" Míra yelled, her shoulder against my arm as her magic flared, knocking down one man after another.

They didn't have magic, so they fell just like Dominoes. They tumbled one after another as they were knocked unconscious when our magic hit them. It took far less time and energy than it should have to take them all out.

In a matter of minutes the flow of soldiers had stopped coming, and Míra and I stood in the center of dozens of unconscious men.

"Why do I have a bad feeling about how easy that was?" Míra whispered, turning to stare through the window Joclyn had taken Ilyan through. "I mean, do we know that was Ilyan?"

She brought up a good point, except the greeting really was restricted to something that would only happen between Ilyan and Jos.

I nodded. "We're sure."

"So why guard their stupid 'God' with minions? Even the guys in Trafalgar Square had magic."

She was right, they had. I hated how spot on she was. This whole thing stunk.

"Where is Thom in his attack?" I asked, but she just shrugged.

"No clue, I left when you guys did. They should just be getting there though." She looked at her phone, clicking the clock on before she pocketed it. Her eyes were wide as she looked at me. "That's where the Kyō army is."

My heart felt like a rock in my chest, every muscle coiled as I tried to temper the rage and panic that was weaving through me.

"What do you... how?" I stuttered in a building panic.

"They knew we went to the SSU after Ilyan. They knew we would come for him, and they didn't expect us to find this place. So, yes, best guess, every single member of their army with magic is in Tokyo. And Thom is going to face them all." Míra gave a low whistle. Damn I picked the wrong battle. All the good stuff is happening there."

"I would refrain from calling all of our people going in against a massive magical army 'the good stuff.'" I raised my eyebrow at her, but she just looked at me with all the beautiful smug glory she usually had.

"We can argue that stuff later, but for now what do you say we go and join the party." She held her hand out to me. I didn't even look at it.

"If you think I am going to let you Stutter me over there, you have another thing coming. Have you forgotten what happened last time?" I was firm, even as her smile was spreading. I wanted to grab her shoulders, to find a way to keep her here and safe, but I already knew that was impossible. Besides, I had a good feeling that if I touched her she would just try to pull me into a Stutter with her anyway.

"I survived." She shrugged, and I thankfully restrained the irate growl that I wanted to direct at her. "I did though! Yes, it took me a bit to wake up, but I did. And if you have taught me anything it's that magic only gets better with practice."

She jutted her hand at me. Of course she would turn my

words on me. I couldn't help but be exceptionally proud of her and thoroughly annoyed at the same time.

"If it fails, Ry, you can just fly me out of there. But if it doesn't, we can help Thom." Her voice had gotten soft. I knew she wanted to get to the fight, but I think part of her wanted to help Thom and the others just as much.

Family still trumped her bloodlust.

Which is probably why I still didn't take her hand. I just stared at her, awed by her, and also desperately needing to find a way to protect her.

"Come on, Ry! At the very least we need to help them. I'm not leaving you here, so unless you plan to stutter out of here yourself…" she was prodding, and she very clearly thought she had won.

Any other time, she probably would have. She was definitely right, you didn't get better at magic without practice. I needed to get there, I needed to help my brother, and there really was only one way to do that.

"Yes, I will," I said, letting all the rage and volatile energy of what Thom was walking into float to the surface. "I *will* Stutter out of here."

I was serious, determined, even if my entire stomach was threatening to turn inside out and explode over everything.

"You can't be serious," Míra said, clearly not believing me.

"I'll see you there, Míra." I grinned, tapping her nose as my magic surged. Even through the wave of nerves, I straightened my shoulders, muscles flexing in panic as I did as Joclyn had instructed me a hundred times.

I focused on my destination. Focus on the place, or the person, and let yourself step into them. Into the suffocating blindness of a Stutter.

For the first time, I did, and I did not look back.

26

WYN

"WE WILL BE FLYING STRAIGHT THERE and into battle. There will be no prep, no marching. Just go in and start taking them down!" Thom's voice echoed over the stone hallway as I raced toward him. The deep, grumpy snarl that was distinctly his somehow fit his current role as a military commander perfectly.

I turned the last corner toward the main hall where everyone was supposed to be gathering and immediately hit a standstill. The halls were just as clogged with people as the main room was, so many people were ready to leave. Ready to fight.

Thom had only sent the call to battle out five minutes ago. He was right, they were antsy.

And I was really freaking jealous.

"Stay with your regional leaders. Be smart. Be safe. If you get hurt, come back to Imdalind. Now go!"

You had to hand it to him, he didn't beat around the bush. He got everyone in there in record time, and now they were all racing out the main exit so fast that in only seconds I was able to make it into the main hall.

Thankfully, Thom was still there. He stood on the bit of raised rock I had left in the center of the space. There used to be a statue there years ago, but now there was just Thom, talking to two of the Skříteks before they too took off. With how fast everyone was moving they would be to Tokyo in minutes.

"Hey! Got room for one more!" I yelled up to Thom as I reached the base of the rock. He turned, clearly ready to welcome anyone into the fight. His face fell the second he saw me, however.

"We talked about this, Wyn." He jumped off the rock platform, already making his way toward the large stretch of rock that everyone else was vanishing into.

"Yes, we talked about it last night when I was sick to my stomach. I'm fine now. I don't want you to be out there alone." I grabbed his arm, pulling him around to face me. He didn't look upset, he looked worried. His hand was far too cold when he put it over mine. I must be running a fair bit hotter than I usually did.

Yet another reason why I needed to be out there.

"I'm not alone, I have thousands of the Chosen with me, and Míra, wherever she went..." He was a fool if he thought he was going to get away with it that easily.

"You know what I mean."

"Wyn. We talked about this." He moved his hand from my arm to my belly, his lips pulling up into a pained smile.

Damn it. Why did he have to play the uterus demon card?

"This is the last war, Thom, I want to--"

"I'll make you a deal. If, in a hundred years there hasn't been another good battle, I'll start a land war for you." He was dead serious. I couldn't help but laugh.

"You'll start a war, just so I can go kill people?" Why was his irrationality so adorable?

"I love you enough to start a war, Wyn. But don't let that go to your head." He grinned, leaning forward to kiss me as his hand grew warm against my stomach, whatever magic was inside of me swelling to find his. "Besides, in a hundred years you and little Cail can go off and fight together."

I think my heart might have stopped. "Cail?"

He shrugged, "I liked your brother. Cail was a good guy. We shouldn't let what Edmund did to him tarnish his legacy."

Fuck. Now I was crying, just standing there sobbing like a blubbering clown.

"Damn you, I can't go into battle like this." I smacked his arm playfully but he just smiled and kissed my nose.

"Good." It was as good as an 'I love you' to Thom who promptly turned and ran out of the entryway. He didn't even look back. Just as we always did years ago.

Every time we were sent out on some mission, we would just leave. No farewell, no heartbreaking last look. He would just leave, then I would leave. But this time I was frozen to the spot.

I stood there, waiting like some lovesick war widow for him to return.

I don't even know how long I stood there when someone else flew through the stone wall of the entrance, this time going the opposite way. Two figures, a smaller one carrying a much larger one.

"Ilyan!" I was rushing to them before they even landed. Joclyn was carrying him like some kind of oversized, super tall infant. If it wasn't for the fact that he was with Joclyn I probably wouldn't have recognized him at all. "What did they do to you?"

"Oh, only tortured me." He said it with the same voice that was strictly Ilyan, the mockery that both of his brothers had, but I had missed from him. He couldn't even stand as Joclyn helped him to the floor, her magic surging as she both checked for injuries and sent a line of magic down the hall.

"Well, you're home now," Joclyn said, kissing him on every inch of skin she could reach. He smiled weakly but kissed her back, both of them doing that creepy stare thing they always did.

"Where's Ryland?" I said after a moment, scanning the rock as though he would come through at any moment. There was nothing.

"He and Míra should be right behind us," Joclyn said, helping Ilyan to his feet as the Chosen and Skřítek she had called from the med ward zoomed into the hall. The Skřítek immediately went into overzealous excitement at seeing Ilyan. The poor Chosen looked as lost as I felt.

"Míra was supposed to go with Thom." My heart turned to lead and dropped to my toes. "She was supposed to be his second."

"And surprise, surprise she followed us." Now Joclyn was looking at the wall, lips pursed and brow furrowed as no one came through the wall and she realized what I did. As the minutes ticked by and they didn't return.

"They are still there."

"You need to go back," Ilyan said, his weak voice still powerful enough to pull our focus. He stood on shaky legs, staring down from where the Skřítek supported him. "You need to finish this."

Joclyn rolled her eyes in true overdramatic fashion as she faced him, clearly ready to fight him. I don't know why she was though. He was right. We needed to help.

"I can't leave you, I just found you." Joclyn rushed back to him, the same pain she was feeling accosting me. Thom may not be alone, but Míra had abandoned him none-the-less. Oh, she was gonna get a whooping when I found her.

"We already talked about this, Joclyn," he whispered, pressing the back of her hand to his lips. "I'll be here when you get back. You have to go. Finish this, mi lasko."

They were having a good old fashioned stare down, so I

looked away, back to the stone wall that no one was traveling in and out of now. If she didn't go, I would.

Thankfully, Joclyn nodded, immediately turning to me.

"Ready?"

She didn't have to ask me twice. Part of me knew I should fight her, tell her I couldn't or make some excuse about how tired I was. But, I really, really wanted to. Plus, I was being commanded by my Queen. Thom would just have to get over himself.

"Where too?" I asked, cracking my neck as Joclyn held out her hand.

I could Stutter on my own, but I had a feeling she might be showing off, just a little bit. So I grinned, took her hand and laughed as she blew Ilyan a kiss and we both vanished into the Stutter.

We reemerged in the middle of a war.

Magic flew in all directions, explosions ripping the world apart as two armies converged under the shadow of the tallest, thinnest building I had ever seen. It stuck out of the earth like a needle made of white scaffolding. From where we were, it looked like it went on forever.

"What the? Where are we?"

"We should be where Ryland and Míra are. They should be here!" Joclyn shouted over the battle, both of us blocking a few attacks as I tried to figure out where we were and who we were fighting.

It was only when ruined magic from one direction, and healthy magic from another intersected right above my head that I realized where we were.

"The Kyō," we said together, looking to the top of the tower that I now recognized as the homebase where Thom had taken the armies.

The Tokyo Sky Tree.

It didn't take me long to find him, hair flying, magic blazing as he fought more than ten of the Kyō's men alone.

"Oh no you don't," I snarled, running toward him as my fire flared, ripping through the air and taking down every Kyō soldier between us. He turned, gruff exterior already in place.

"Wyn, I told you--" He stopped when Jos came up beside me, his eyes wide as he asked the question that he had been waiting for years to hear the answer to. He was so focused on asking her his silent question that he missed the attack zooming right by his head.

Luckily for him and his brains I had come along.

"Your brother is fine." Joclyn was practically beaming at that, and Thom erupted in joy as he took down the Kyō soldier that was rushing up behind him without even looking.

"Great! Now let's get home so I can tell him what a douchebag he is!" Thom raged, grinning from ear to ear as he turned, attacking one soldier just as I turned another to dust.

"Why don't we go in there?" I called, fighting off another attacker as more soldiers streamed through the door at the base of the building.

"The whole building is shielded. I am sure whoever is behind all of this is right there, but we can't get in, and I can't get close enough to try to puncture it! Wanna break it down Wyn?" Thom asked, the three of us standing before it as I smiled and let the fire erupt from the palm of my hands.

"Gladly."

27

RYLAND

I WAS DYING.

This was worse than Ilyan's barrier around the cathedral in Prague, worse than every other time that Joclyn had taken me through the Stutter. I was fairly certain that I was going to come out on the other side with a missing limb given how much pain was radiating through my bones.

Emerging on the other side, I fell to the ground heaving as I tried to catch my breath and keep the contents of my stomach on the inside. I did a quick check of limbs, thankfully I hadn't lost any.

I possibly should not have been so dramatic, but I had yet to open my eyes. For all I knew I was trapped on some mountain top, or in some subdimension where everyone had ears the size of their arms.

I took one last calming breath, grateful when my stomach settled and I could open my eyes without the world spinning underneath me. Not that what I opened my eyes to was any better.

There was nothing below me.

Nothing but miles of free air and white scaffolding. I wasn't falling, but my magic wasn't keeping me in place either. I was stuck on my hands and knees, watching the sparks of a battle on the streets far below.

"What the hell?" I asked as I scuttled back, grateful when the miles of nothing turned out to be a layer of glass.

"There you are!" Míra yelled from behind me as she appeared with a pop, standing firmly on the metal part of the floor. It must have been some kind of glass observation deck. "I was honestly afraid you were gonna get stuck in there."

She was trying to be cocky, but her worry showed through as she practically yanked me to my feet, her arms already wrapped around me.

"Good job not dying," she whispered, everything else that she wanted to say caught in the intensity of the hug as I wrapped my arms around her, pressing my lips to her hair.

"I'm glad you're okay too." It was just a whisper, but it could have been a whip with how she jumped back, straightening her jeans and jacket as though they were covered in dirt. For a moment, every inch of her was awkward teenager.

"Okay! Let's go finish this!" And she was back to business. I guess we would have to address all that later. "Should we find Thom?"

I wanted to say yes, it was why we had come here after all. But I had a feeling we had somehow Stuttered right where we needed to be.

"No." I stepped back onto the glass bottomed floor, staring down at the eruptions of magic and flame that were exploding everywhere. Based on what I was seeing down there Míra wasn't the only one to have shown up where they weren't expected.

"If I had to guess, this is the Sky Tree in the center of Tokyo. From what Thom found out, this is where the Kyō headquarters are. So, whoever is leading them is somewhere in this tower."

"Perfect." Míra stood beside me, both of us looking down as

one explosion turned into another, a ripple of blasts encircling the building. Everything below us was on fire. I braced myself, half expecting the building to topple, but instead the air around it shimmered as whatever shield had been keeping them all out fell away.

Seconds later, the entire building filled with the sound of alarms, the tremors of stomping feet rippling through the line of doors behind us.

"Damn. We have perfect timing, don't we?" Míra turned toward the noise, her grin as bright as the magic that was already encircling her fingers.

"And I guess good aim. I've never known a wicked king not to sit on top of his throne." I pulled my magic up, both of us ready to race out of this room and into whatever hell was waiting for us on the other side.

"Good thing we both have practice ending wicked kings." Míra grinned at me, and I couldn't help myself, I laughed.

She was right. It seemed fitting it would be the two of us ending yet another evil overlord.

Of course, the first time we had been little more than enemies. Now? I restrained the need to kiss her and turned toward the door. Míra was already racing toward it.

I actually wasn't sure if the girl was afraid of anything.

She blasted through the room with a scream, the door flying off its hinges and directly into a poor unsuspecting soldier who was thrown into the opposite wall.

"That's one!" Míra yelled, already sending an attack toward the line of soldiers that were racing down the hall.

These were not the soldiers from Mongolia. These ones had magic and were already attacking us. Lines of rotten magic went everywhere. It spiraled into the walls and ceiling as we pushed it away, the weak power fizzling out with barely more than a glance from ours.

"Two!"

"Are we really going to keep count?" I yelled, darting away as an attack whizzed by the side of my head. The slither of broken magic collided with the wall behind me and cracked it.

"Three! And, yes we are," Míra called back, already moving from her third victim to the next. She was moving so fast I was going to be left picking off whatever of the Kyō she couldn't get.

Which wouldn't be all bad, if she wasn't keeping score.

"One!" I yelled, slamming a dark haired attacker down the hall and away from us. He had only been seconds away from attacking Míra and there was no way in hell I was going to let that fly. "I don't see the point of this! Two!"

"Four! Five!" Míra yelled in return, flashing me a smile before she spun around, hair flinging around her as she took down number five. "Fine, I'll make it worth your while."

"How?" I flung magic back just as I shoved another man forward, right into a door that swung open to reveal at least ten other guards. Great. "Five!"

I would say I was catching up, but with how Míra's magic was sparking behind me I didn't know if that was possible. She was a firestorm, taking down attacks and attackers as though it was nothing more than a game. I raced behind her, magic sparking and flaring over the ceiling and walls as I shocked a few more to the ground.

The sound of the battle was attracting more and more of these guys, although oddly none of them seemed to be very well trained. They had magic, they just didn't know how to use it.

"If you get more points than me I'll give you a kiss." She grinned, and I both hated and loved how my stomach swooped at that. "Plus I'll throw in a hundred point bonus for whoever takes out the head of the snake."

"Eight! And what if you win?" I asked, perfectly content to ignore the prize she had set for me.

"I get to tell everyone that I killed the bad guy *and* did better than you in battle. Oh, and thirteen." She looked at me, eyes alight as she took down yet another with ease, the same training that I had as a child showing through.

Sometimes I needed the reminder that my father had trained both of us. We were both ruthless.

"Fine. You're on. But I'm not holding back."

"Good, you're going to need it to catch up." She blew me a kiss and turned back to the waves of soldiers that were racing down the hall toward us.

I picked off the soldiers that streamed out of the room with ease, one after another they squeezed through the door with a shout, ready to end me. One after another I sent them down to the ground.

Magic sparked in blasts of color as Míra's laugh echoed over us, mixing with the battle cry of the Kyō in a creepy symphony that was made more horrifying by the explosions that rippled off the walls. In only a few minutes, everything silenced, leaving Míra and me standing in a garden of bodies, most only paralyzed.

"Thirty-one," Míra said as we charged forward, heading in the direction the soldiers had been coming from.

"Twenty-eight." I ignored the wrinkled-nose grin she gave me. She could rub it in later, if she won. For now I still had a chance to catch up.

"What do you think? Were they running toward the armies below or toward their master to protect him?" Míra looked either way down the hall, toward where the soldiers had come, and where they were headed.

I stepped into the hall, facing the direction the soldiers were headed, toward the high stairs to the tower and the throb of magic that was sitting there. A monster on top of their high tower. A pulse of power echoed down to me, the waves of it so familiar that it almost took my breath away.

"They're up there." Whoever they were.

Míra followed me without question, both of us racing toward the low pulse of magic as though we were charging toward the final boss in the video game.

The halls were strangely empty, probably because everyone who had been here had come running to face us. The faint sounds of battle echoed through the halls behind us as the armies from below slowly made their way up the tower, but other than that it was nothing and no one but Míra and me as we raced up the last of the stairs and to the door at the end.

It swung open before we could even reach it, revealing a well-dressed man and a walking stick we both knew all too well. He sat in a single chair in the middle of the room, the high-back wooden thing obviously pulled away from the desk in the corner so he could watch us enter.

He was waiting for us.

A tyrant on a throne at the top of his tower.

"Suji."

28

RYLAND

"Suji." We said together, mine a gasp, Míra's a snarl.

I had burned Suji to a crisp, but I guess Míra had missed that seeing as she had been unconscious and then carted to the other side of the world. It was time to fill her in.

"I killed you," I snapped as the man looked up at me, a wide greasy grin already taking over his features.

I pulled Míra back, my arm firm around her bicep as I cemented her to me.

"You're not Suji." I let my magic boil, pulling it right under my skin in preparation for whatever this man was going to send at us. Míra did the same, her magic buzzing against mine as she yanked her arm out of my grip and tried to protect me, just as I was trying to protect her. I had a feeling that this was going to become a thing for us.

"No," the man said, walking stick swinging as he rose from the chair. "I am his brother, Chikara. I am the one who leads the Kyō, and the one that will kill you for revenge."

"Well, aren't you delightful," Míra said, still angling herself in front of me no matter how many times I tried to push her away. "No 'nice to meet you'. No 'monologuing about your evil plan'. Just die! I'll take it!"

Míra attacked without so much as a howl of warning, her magic soaring from the palm of her hand and right toward the old man. He didn't even flinch. Before the magic could even reach him, the tip of his cane ignited, a bright flare soaring in all directions that zapped away Míra's attack as though it had never existed.

"You foolish Gods. You think you can take my throne from me. A God gifted me with this power and I will not let you take it from me so easily!"

"Ugh. Here we go again with the god talk," I groaned, even though I hadn't missed that what this man said was different from what his brother said. Suji wanted to worship me. Chikara clearly had other plans. "Torturing a man does not *give* you power. It makes you a tyrant."

"A man?" Chikara said, swinging his staff around and sending a few sparks out of the tip. "Do you mean the God we rescued from the SSU?" He paused, grinning with all the slickness I had seen from his brother. I braced for what came next. This would not be good. "No. Not him. His sister was the one who taught me of the power of the gods. She was the one I took my strength from. What was her name?"

"Ovailia." Míra had stopped fighting me. Some of that playful light was gone from her eyes as she looked at the man and his spinning staff. "What did you do to her?"

"I didn't kill her if that's what you're asking. No. She was already dead when I found her, screaming at the end of an alley. Everyone was concerned about the man, thinking he had been bitten, but Suji and I only saw her. We took her in. We kept her alive as the heart she conjured for herself gave out. I guess she gave her heart to another, quite literally." He laughed, but the sound was harsh and angry. It scratched against my soul as everything he was saying fell into place, and everything Míra had been saying for years became truth. Ovailia *had* saved Ilyan in the end.

"We even sacrificed our sister to the bite of a Vilỳ so she could help. But even that didn't work, which was fine, I suppose. I got what I needed from her in the end." I could only stare at him as he flipped the staff again, magic stretching to the end of the room in a line of sparks.

The sparks of the magic that felt familiar. Now, I knew why.

It was Ovailia's magic.

I didn't know how he did it, and I didn't care. Only one thing was pulsing through me now. Ovailia had sacrificed herself for Ilyan, and this man had killed her. This man had taken her magic, and figured out how to take the magic of others.

"Well, I guess we found who we are supposed to kill." I stepped forward, Míra by my side, as we faced the man and his twisted smile.

"I wish you luck," was all he said before he pointed the staff right at us and sent a stream of glittering white across the room.

Míra sent up a shield, but the second the magic intersected with his, it fell away in lines of fire, the attack still on a beeline for us. We darted out of the way, both of us falling to the floor as Míra dodged one way and I another. Chikara laughed as I stared at Míra, her face screwed up in determination as she looked from him to me.

"Looks like someone needs his dick cut off." She jumped up, rushing the man and leaving me sputtering on the floor.

I really shouldn't be surprised about anything that girl does or says.

She raced over the floor, running to the other side of the room so that Chikara was between us. She separated us and Chikara's focus as he continued to swing the staff.

"Do you really think that will work?" he asked, clearly not

seeing what I had. Míra may be on the other side of the room from me, but her magic was not. It spiraled behind him, unseen by him as he darted his focus between what he thought were his only two enemies. Me and Míra.

"Oh, no," Míra said with a laugh. "I just wanted to see how dumb you were."

Míra jumped into the air, yelling like some kind of warrior as she went high and her magic spiraled like a Catherine wheel over the ground. I stayed where I was, hands out as my magic soared from me and I flooded the entire space with dark fog.

I only got a glimpse of Chikara's horrified face before the blackness swarmed him. Míra screamed as both she and her magic intersected with the man.

I raced forward, pulling my magic around me and her in a shield as the black began to break apart, and the fighting pair before me came back into view. The staff had deflected the Catherine wheel of Míra's magic, leaving her fighting him head on.

Her plan may not have worked, but thanks to the black fog he was oblivious to my arrival from behind. I grabbed him, my arm circling around his neck as I pressed my hand against his back and let my magic spark directly into his bones.

He screamed, the high pitched shriek echoing over the walls as Míra stepped back, grinning in victory. I moved my other hand out, ready to restrain him when he swung the stick around and slammed the tip into my forearm.

The skin burned as whatever magic was in the stick cut into me, flesh searing as it was cut apart and what felt like knives zinged through my body. Screaming in pain, I dropped him and staggered back, already shooting a misaimed attack back at the man who was flinging the stick around again.

Lines of light sped from the tip, launching toward both me and Míra, and she was pissed.

"How dare you!" With a scream, she raced at him, vanishing from view with the slightest pop. Usually a Stutter was best used as a distraction, but Míra went right to him, reappearing on his back. She clung to him like a koala, screaming as she slammed her hands onto his head. A kill shot.

She didn't get too far before Chikara flung the staff back, aiming right for her face. Sparks flew everywhere as she grabbed the tip of the wood with her hand, magic erupting around her palm.

"And you thought you were going to get revenge?" She laughed, still plastered to his back, the staff clasped in her hand.

He hadn't even noticed that I was standing. That my magic was already soaring right toward him. He had no way to dodge, no way to fight back as the powerful attack slammed into his gut. Míra took off into the air as he was thrown back, right into the glass wall. It cracked but did not break as he slid down it, the staff in two pieces by his feet.

"Is he--?" I began, Míra's attack zooming past me before I could even finish asking. It hit him right between the eyes.

"If he wasn't before, he is now." Yes, she really had spent too much time around Wyn.

Although, in situations like this I really wasn't going to question it.

"Since I killed him, does that mean I won the hundred points?" I panted, my hand flat against my arm where the bleeding had thankfully begun to slow.

"Did you kill him? I'm pretty sure it was a group effort." Míra was heaving as much as I was.

Her skin was sticky with sweat, her face flushed and streaked with blood.

Yet, somehow, she was the most beautiful thing I had ever seen.

"I got the last hit. I'll take the victory." God, I hated that I was fighting this. I hated more that I was trying to win for one reason only.

"Admit it. You just want to kiss me," Míra teased, I guess she figured me out.

"Oh fuck it," I breathed, grabbing her around the waist and pressing her right against me. She grinned at me with all the saucy victory she possessed before she was the one to lean in and press her lips against mine.

Fireworks rocked through me, hungry need pulsing as I lifted her off the floor and held her, letting my touch devour her.

Míra's lips danced alongside mine as her arms clung to me, her hands tangling in my hair as all of the glass in the high office exploded.

She giggled before kissing me again, her touch hungry and needy and wonderful.

"Well, I guess I should have seen this coming," Joclyn said from right behind us. We both stiffened, Míra giving me another kiss before she slid from my arms and we turned to face not just Joclyn, but Thom and Wyn who stood in the doorway.

We hadn't even heard the door open.

"Took you guys long enough," Míra laughed, hands on her hips. "I had to kill that guy without you. What would you do without me?"

29

RYLAND

"ARE YOU READY FOR THIS, your majesty?"

I glared at Wyn, who was grinning at me in full awareness of what she was doing. She knew what was waiting for me on the other side of those doors, and she knew just how much I was dreading it.

But I had chosen this. I promised both Ilyan and Joclyn this, if only for a few years while Ilyan recovered.

And part of me knew it was right.

It was still just sitting very heavy on my chest.

We had only returned from the battle with the Kyō a week ago, and while I would love to say the world was promptly put back in order, it had only been thrown apart.

There was no leadership, and wars were bound to flourish again. Someone had to take control, and as much as Wyn wanted to be Queen Empress of the world, she had bowed out at the last minute.

"Aw, c'mon, you'll do great!" It was Míra who threw her arm around my neck, giving me just as big of a smile as Wyn was. Those two were trouble, there was no way around that.

"Don't think you are getting a tad bit too excited?" I asked. She just smiled broader.

If it wasn't for what I was about to head into I would say that those two were up to something.

I gave them one last look before staring into the mess of ribbon in my hand and nodding to Wyn and Thom, who threw the door open with flourish.

"I present to you, the youngest son of Edmund LaRue, brother to Ilyan Krul, and our King, Ryland LaRue."

Wyn's voice rang out as I gave Míra one last look, the girl smiling as I slid the ribbon over my hand, securing it on my wrist as I walked into the hall.

The massive space was full of the Chosen, of Trpaslíks, and Skřítek; more of which had come to our side after the Kyō had fallen.

They stood, staring at me, and as one they clapped their hands above their heads.

As one, we walked into a new world together.

As I stared at them, I couldn't help but be just a little excited. There was a lot to do, more than enough things in this broken down world to repair.

But we could. We would find a way, together.

No matter how scared out of my mind I was, it was the hope that kept me going, and that was something we all had in common.

"I accept."

30

ILYAN

She had been wrapped in my arms for the past few months, neither of us willing to let go. We had slept in a tangle of limbs and sheets, never getting enough of each other. Our days were spent curled together in playful curves, talking about everything that had happened, everything we had missed.

I absorbed everything she had to tell me, every story and every memory. While it had taken me a few days to open up about what happened to me, it felt good to share, to tell her of the fear and pain, and to know that I was not alone.

That she was there.

And that she understood.

While not the same, she had been driven to madness while trapped in Cail's mind. Driven to an insanity that even I didn't reach. She knew the pain of that type of misery, of that torture. It made sharing easier, it made healing safer. It had been my love that held her while she had found her feet, and it would be her love that would help me find mine.

Seeing her dedication to me, that support, brought even more love into my heart. Into us.

Of course, that connection was made all the more amazing by the return of my magic.

It had been that kiss, right before she left to help with the Kyō, when it all came flooding back.

Like a bolt of lightning it sparked, pushing through like an explosion that I barely kept restrained. Jos and Wyn had already gone off to fight, and I had far too much healing for my body to catch up on anyway.

When she returned I swept my mate into my arms, announced I had a lifetime to catch up on, and rushed her away to the house in France that we both spent way too much time dreaming about. Thank goodness it was still standing.

We hadn't left since.

Of course, we have had visitors, but most of the time we were alone; curled up under blankets, or cuddled together on the big squishy chairs on the balcony as we lost ourselves in each other.

Right now, however, as the sun dipped below the horizon and everything was covered in gold, we lay in our usual tangle, listening to each other's heartbeats.

What did you miss the most? Joclyn asked into my mind, her voice soft and hesitant as she curled deeper into me. The texture of her voice made it clear that she was drifting back to sleep again, the slow steady beat of her breathing cementing the fact.

"Sunlight," I answered without hesitation. Whispering my answer aloud as she sighed.

She had asked me that question multiple times over the last few days, and every time I gave her a different answer. It was a joke that I had become obsessed with teasing her over. She could see the answer in my mind anyway.

She chuckled and burrowed herself into me, just as a soft knock on the door pulled my focus.

One flare of my magic told me who it was, and while years

ago I may have been concerned with letting him see us like this, now it didn't matter.

"Enter," I called, the loud command in my voice making Joclyn jump.

"With a voice like that you'll be claiming your crown again soon," Ryland teased as he stepped into the room, his voice light and calm as he shut the door behind him.

"I am sorry to disappoint you, brother, but I don't see that happening anytime soon." I made sure to keep my voice lower this time.

Ryland's sigh was obvious as he sat down on the foot of the bed, his movements careful in an attempt not to disrupt us. The motion caused Joclyn to press closer to me, something I would not complain over.

"You promised me ten years, and that is what I will give you. Any more than that and I will simply bribe you," he said. "I do not know how you ruled for so long, and so well."

"It was not always perfect, and I needed my breaks as well," I admitted, the memories of the time I had spent in the monastery, or building this house, or remodeling Rioseco making so much more sense now. "You will have to find time for yourself as well."

"I'm afraid I haven't mastered that yet," he sighed, his blue eyes laughing as he ran his hand through his hair. "Maybe I'll do that right after I finish convincing Australia's new government to stand with us."

I chuckled lightly at that, his own frustration tickling his lips as he sighed and leaned against the massive footboard, looking from me to Joclyn as though this was nothing more than an everyday occurrence.

"Is she asleep?" he finally asked, the lack of disdain, anger, and ownership still catching me off guard.

"She is doing a very good job of pretending to be," I answered, just as the girl in question let out a very large snore.

The sound made both Ryland and I laugh, although Jos refused to move, instead curling against me in an attempt to hide her chuckles.

"Well, you might want to wake her up for this," Ryland prodded, his eyes dancing in delight as whatever secret he had come in here hiding threatened to explode. "I have news."

"It better be good news," Joclyn mumbled, Ry didn't even hesitate to answer.

"The best."

Jos sighed, groaned, pressed one last kiss against my neck and slowly turned, her eyes already shooting daggers at Ryland.

"I was almost asleep, you know."

"You are still wearing your clothes, Jos." His banter was meant for her, but I laughed right along with him, leaving poor Joclyn with the difficult decision of who to glower at.

In the end, she chose me, poking me in the ribs as she teased me right back. "You let in a straight up loon."

"I'd be careful what you say," I hissed as I ran my fingers up her side in an obvious attempt at tickling. "You never know how much of that runs in the family."

"Who says..."

"I have news!" Ryland announced again, his voice loud as he pulled us out of our bubble.

The look he gave us was such a cross between the powerful king and the frustrated kid brother that I couldn't help but laugh, the joy expelling from me in a loud burst that caused Joclyn to jump and Ryland to scowl deeper.

His curls bounced as he shook his confusion away, turning to us with a piercing blue stare as he looked right at me. "We found her."

It was all he needed to say.

We had been searching for Kaye for months, seeing as the other tracking light on the webpage had led not to Kaye, but to some old man in Spain.

My heartbeat sped up, Joclyn's accelerating to match as she fell away from me, my still weak legs pushing me to stand beside the bed, bare chest, loose pajama pants and all.

"Where?" I heard Joclyn ask behind me in exhilaration.

Ryland mumbled something as the sound of crumpling paper pulled me back to them, the two curled over a map that Ry had obviously pulled out of a book.

"Sweden," Ryland stated. "Sigtuna to be exact. I have never heard of it, but Wyn said..."

"Yes. I owned the first inn there. A tiny thing. We used it as a safe house for many years..."

I drifted off as the memories hit me, moments in time that were almost lost.

"Yes, well," Ryland cleared his throat as he pulled me back, Joclyn's hand wrapping around my own in understanding. "Wyn said you would know this intersection." Again another smile. "Which is the closest thing to where she is: here."

The map crinkled as he released it onto the bed, the corners rolling as he dug in his pockets. Shoving a nicely folded square of paper toward me, Ryland looked from me to Joclyn in anticipation.

I couldn't respond. Luckily, Joclyn jumped up and wrapped her arms around Ryland's neck, thanking him over and over as I began to unfold the paper and reveal an address in loopy feminine handwriting.

Kaye.

She was here. She was right here.

I could find here. I could thank her.

"Thank you, Ryland," I whispered, my own thanks echoing

Joclyn's as I clenched the paper in my fist, suddenly determined to locate some regular clothes.

"You are very welcome, both of you," Ryland said, peeling Joclyn away as he took a step toward the door. "I have some issues I must attend to, but call me when you have her. I would like to meet her too. And Jos, Ilyan; I wouldn't wait too long. It seems she moves around a lot."

"Thanks, Ry," Jos said from behind me as he left, her voice distant as I began to make my way over to my dresser.

It was a curse I had grumbled about many times before. My now returned magic could do everything it had before, but no magic could make muscle grow. That was on me, and the slow healing of my atrophied appendages was only angering me.

"In five years it will only be a memory," Jos whispered as she stepped past me, her hand soft against my arms.

"I would rather it not take that long." I almost regretted saying it aloud, the anger and frustration was not really like me.

Joclyn responded with a knowing smile and a chuckle inside of my head. "With an attitude like that, it should only take one, then."

It took some time, but I was able to get dressed for the first time in years, pajamas having been my uniform since returning home. Pants, shirt, shoes, jacket, they all fit. The slender attire matched the braid Joclyn had put in my hair. The plait, the outfit, they filled me with an odd pride I hadn't expected.

It looked as though no time had passed.

Just as though I had a bad dream... nothing more.

"We are going to need to pick up a few magazines," Jos said with a wink, her hands soft as they straightened the jacket. "You look a little out of date."

Except for that.

I cringed. Jos gave me a soft smile that perfectly echoed what was on my mind, her eyes sad as she lifted onto her tiptoes and pulled me down into a kiss.

Her lips were soft as they pressed into mine, the pressure an intense power as our magic sparked. Warmth rushed through me, the lights of a million different hues breaking through the air. I saw them for just a moment, the colors fading as her kiss did, although she did not move away from me.

"But you still look like my Ilyan," she whispered, her breath gentle and warm against my lips. "I couldn't ask for anything more."

"You are my everything, my mate."

"And you are mine," she whispered right into my mind, the words beautiful as she sang them in my native tongue.

"Even though we may be a little outdated," I whispered the words in Czech and she giggled, the sound light as she finally pulled away, grabbing the paper from where I had placed it on the dresser and turned to me.

"Well, what do you say we go get the person who gave us the opportunity to be just that?"

Her smile expanded as I put my hand in hers, and with one swell of her magic she pulled us through the darkness of the world under ours, and right to that quaint little intersection in Sweden, right where my magic and memories guided her.

Everything about the place was different. While some of the buildings looked similar, not one was the same. The streets were paved and the crowded sidewalks looked strangely out of place against the hundred-year-old buildings.

But there was one thing they couldn't change, the smell of the fish against the salty sea air. I smelled it with a delight I hadn't experienced in over two hundred years. Joclyn, however, crinkled her nose in disgust and exhaled sharply, trying to ignore the pungent smell.

The look on her face was one that gave me more of a desire

to laugh.

"Now who is outdated," I teased and grabbed the paper from her, took one glance and began to lead her down the street to our left.

Old homes and businesses were set against modern conveniences. I had seen this juxtaposition in cities for centuries, perhaps it hadn't bothered me because I had watched the change happen. But seeing this beautiful little village like this was jarring.

Two left turns, a right, and a quick trip down an alley brought us to a street lined with trees, backed up against a massive field. Between the street and field was a line of tiny cottage houses, the thatched roofs and sloped windows exactly what I had expected to see from this ancient village.

I breathed deep, a surreal feeling of home hitting against my chest as we walked past the first two, and turned to face the third.

It was a tiny thing. With white shutters and porcelain blue stucco, it looked like it was right out of a storybook. It was beautiful.

But mostly, it was safe. It looked like a home.

I could tell at once why she had chosen it.

"Are you ready?" Joclyn asked from beside me, her hand a tight vice around my own.

I could only nod as together, we walked up to the door. Joclyn rapped on the door so fast I wasn't sure if it was a knock or the sound of my heart in my ears.

I had been in situations like this before. While the anxiety I felt now was nothing near the moment that I had seen Joclyn for the first time, sitting at a battered old desk in school, it was at least in the top twenty.

"I like that memory too," Joclyn whispered, running her thumb over my hand just as the door opened and the nut brown eyes of the girl who had given everything to save me looked into me for the first time in years.

I could see the confusion there for only a moment before her hand flew to her mouth, soft sounds of emotion bleeding through her fingers.

"Kaye?" I whispered, my voice broken from tears. "Allow me to introduce myself. My name is Ilyan Krul, and this is my wife, Joclyn.

It's a pleasure to meet you."

31

JOCLYN

SIXTY YEARS LATER

"I don't care what anyone says, I will never, ever tire of watching them take their shirts off. I mean, look at the display of muscle. Yum."

Wyn leaned forward in the padded seats of our usual box, bracelets jangling, chin in her hands as she looked out at the pristine green field. I had seen a lot of Rugby games, but this shirts vs skins situation was adding a whole new level to the game. If only because of who was playing skins.

Wyn was even licking her lips. Too bad we weren't the only ones who had come to watch the game from our designated "royal box". Ugh. Whoever started calling it that should be given a stern talking to. Although knowing my luck it was Ry. And a 'stern talking to' wasn't going to do much more than his rolling his eyes at me and walking away.

"God, Mom, stop. That's beyond gross. I'm going to throw up." Cail leaned around me, the dark eyes he had inherited from Wyn flashing with a touch of blue.

Wyn didn't even turn to him, she was too busy staring at the "skins" team and smacking her lips obnoxiously. I, however, leaned back, pretending to be interested in the game and covering my mouth to hide my smile. Not that I wasn't interested in the game, I had just seen a lot of Rugby in my arguably short life.

Wyn and Cail were just better entertainment.

She always chose something to torment him with, today it happened to be Wyn's obsession with muscle. Whatever gave her the ability to pester her middle-aged son who whines like a child.

"I'm looking at your father, Cail, get a grip." She waved him off and scooted closer, licking her lips again.

"Did you just tell me to 'get a grip'? That phrase is a couple hundred years old, mom. God, you are so weird," Cail scoffed, throwing the ratted old book he was reading back into his backpack. "You do realize that Uncle Ryland and Ilyan are out there don't you? And they aren't wearing shirts either."

"I do, but I am looking at your father. Look at those rippling pectorals. Firm buttocks. MmmMmm." Cail's jaw dropped, and the smile I had been trying to hide peeked out.

Fine, I'll play.

"You better not be looking at the King's firms buttocks, Cail, because I have dibs." I gave him a smile, twisting the long golden ribbon between my fingers, as though he needed the reminder.

"No," Cail snapped, throwing the busted laptop he always carted around in after his book. I was having serious trouble keeping a straight face now. "I'm not going to listen to this again. I refuse."

"You could always go play with them, Cail." I smiled at him, earning myself a glare. "You are almost fifty years old now, honey. You can keep up. Míra's playing."

"Not interested." He looked between the two of us. He may whine like a child at times, but we had done this enough that he knew exactly what was going on.

"Aww come on, even your sister is out there! Be among your

people." Wyn gestured wildly to the field, mass amounts of bracelets jangling and pulling the focus of the Chosen who had clustered in the bleachers around us as they had done for decades. Anything to be closer to the royals. Ugh.

They couldn't hear us thanks to the shield I always put around our box after being eavesdropped on by one too many reporters, but the wild bracelet jangling must have snuck through somehow. I twitched my finger, tightening up the shield and causing the rest of them to turn back to the field where they all were stoically pretending not to be paying attention to everything we were doing.

Yes, being Queen still sucked sometimes.

"After what I just heard, I would rather check myself into one of those mortal retirement homes. Live among people who are more sane than you lot. I can't believe I am stuck with you all for eternity!"

"You could always get married, honey, give me some grandkids. Be stuck with more people for eternity."

"I... can you... ugh!" Cail stormed off, bag over his shoulder as he made his way out of the box and down through the bleachers that were filled with Chosen and the few mortals who had braved their way in here to watch the match. Heads followed him as he grumbled and waved and kept glancing back at us with his dark brooding eyes.

Wyn and I, however, were reduced to giggles. Well, until both Thom and Ilyan turned to give us "the look" and Ryland started laughing. He had to pause the game thanks to a still stubborn Cail who was rushing into the middle of the field and ripping his shirt off. I would be worried that he was going to do something dangerous, but it was Cail.

Instead, he pranced into the middle of the field, displaying his own set of muscles and doing a weird shimmy dance as he yelled up to us. "MmmMmm Muscles! Look mom! Sexy, sexy, muscles!"

Wyn and I collapsed into each other with belly-aching laughter. Even Thom was trying not to laugh. The Chosen however, were looking at us like we had lost it.

Okay, maybe Cail had a point.

By the end of it we were all laughing, Cail included, even though he was being shuffled to the side of the field. He already had his nose buried in his book before Ryland could get control of the situation.

'Exactly what have you and Wyn done now?' Ilyan's voice rattled through my mind, his blue eyes smiling at me from down on the field.

'It had to do with buttocks and you shouldn't dig through the last few minutes,' I warned him, fully aware that he was already doing just that. Judging by the massive grin that was overtaking his already gorgeous face I would say he had watched the whole thing.

'Warned you.'

'You and Wyn really ought to find something else to do with your time,' he said as Ryland blew the whistle and tried to get everything back on track.

'What? Like watch your perfect back muscles as you run, everything rippling and stretching and...' He almost fell on his face, giving me another heartbreaking smile before he closed our connection and went back to the game. Without a war to focus on anymore, Ilyan had thrown himself into Ryland's little experiment wholeheartedly. Sports to help connect what was left of the world. Chosen, Immortals, and Mortals as equals. It had been good for everyone for a while. But lately there had been a chasm opening up between those with magic, and those who were never bitten by the twisted Vilỳ Edmund had made.

I don't think any of us were fooling ourselves about how bad it was getting. Even here none of the mortals or Chosen were sitting together. The number of mortals here had even been cut in half from last year's attendance.

"You're thinking about it again, aren't you?" Wyn said. The crowd cheered for a goal that we had both missed, everyone standing and cheering around us.

"It's hard not to think about. It's a real problem, Wyn." I gestured to the obvious gaps in seating and even the few Chosen who were openly mocking a terrified mortal. Wyn rolled her eyes.

"Spoken like the Queen you are," Wyn sighed, patting my shoulder exaggeratingly. "I am a firm believer that this will sort itself out."

"You do know you are full of shit, right?" I asked, and Wyn actually flinched as though I had punched her, the saucy assassin pursing her lips at me.

"We literally just came out of a thousand-year war--"

"Sixty years is 'just came out of'?" Wyn interrupted me, stealing my thunder.

"No, but we caught the last of the Vilỳ only a few months ago, we are safe for the first time in centuries. And that war we came out of was built on the backs of class disparity."

"Oh god, what library did you find and is that why Cail always has his nose in a book again?" She rambled, genuinely concerned. I gave her a simpering smile, she had totally caught me. "Never mind. I don't want to know."

"We can't let the same thing happen again, Wyn. This whole class system and people thinking they are better than others because they have magic."

"If you are talking about letting those Vilỳ bite everyone from here to the former Republic of China then let me slap that smug smile off your face right now," Wyn snapped. No slapping necessary, the smile was gone. I sighed and leaned back in my chair. I had clearly inadvertently activated Wyn's sassy mode. I could be here a while.

"Giving everyone power only makes things worse," she hissed as the crowd erupted in a scream again, the packed stands rolling into one of those wave things. "Remember the Kyō? And that damn bitch who tortured your husband? Power everywhere puts power in the wrong places and *that's* how thousand-year wars get started. Nu-uh. All the Vilỳ are caught, we know the Chosen bitten by the diseased Vilỳ don't have an extended life, and they can't pass on their powers. In another 50 years they will all be gone. And then magic will be nice and controlled again."

She folded her arms over her chest and leaned back, smug, content, and staring at half naked men.

"So, you want us to be the only ones with power and to rule over the weak, pathetic, mortals like dictators?"

"When you put it that way it sounds awful," Wyn said, shifting in her seat. "But you know we wouldn't be like iron fist, take all your rights away bastards. More like equality managers. And without the Chosen we would have nothing to manage. Everything would be equal."

"Except us."

"Yes. Because we would be like gods. Sexy shirtless gods who are running balls places that we are missing because you are rambling on about diversity trust funds or something."

She was no longer listening to me. Although she did stand and cheer in some weird dance when Thom tackled someone else. No points or score or anything, just Wyn cheering for her husband. Meanwhile, a Chosen man threw a whole cup of soda at a mortal who was quickly getting up to leave.

Holy freaking turtle airplanes. This has to stop.

I was up and ready to charge down there when Wyn put her hand around my firearm, forcing me back into my seat and gesturing toward the guard who was already making his way over there.

"You worry too much."

"Isn't that what Gods are supposed to do? Or are we equality managers?" I asked, my heart keeping pace with Ilyan's steps as he ran across the field. There was something amazing that happened to skin when it was covered with sweat. "Either way it sounds like we would be working in one of those department stores that sells both pudding and dynamite."

"I love those stores," Wyn sighed and sat back. "If you are so worried about it, why don't you reach into your sight and see what we are supposed to do."

"You know it doesn't work like that."

"I do." She folded her legs underneath her, sitting cross legged on her padded chair as she faced me. "But I also know you well enough to know you tried anyway. What did you see?"

"More Chosen." I spoke barely above a whisper, Wyn crinkling her face at me. Yes, I knew I wasn't making any sense. "But they weren't like these guys. They were trained."

"Like an army?" I hadn't thought of it that way, and that was so much worse.

I shook my head. "No, like a school."

"So, you want to start a school? I think the library you and Cail found has gone to your head." She rolled her eyes and turned away from me. "Well, if you do, make sure you make Cail headmaster or something. That kid needs some direction. And a wife. Or a husband."

"That's not a bad idea."

"Wait, you are actually going to do this?" Her eyes were saucers, the dark black irises looking even darker against the whites of her eyes.

"There is power in the world, but it shouldn't be for the few, or those who were lucky enough to get bit. Everyone should have a chance. And if they learn about it, and know how to wield it, maybe we won't get any little Edmunds running around. And maybe we won't get this mess." I gestured toward the stands, hoping to draw my point home, but Wyn was still staring at me with her mouth sagging down to her belly button.

'It really is a good idea, my love,' Ilyan whispered into my mind, giving me a slight smile from the field before his loss of focus ended up getting him tackled to the ground.

'And that's why you should stay out of my head during games.'

'Touché.'

"Besides Wyn," I said slowly, knowing that Ilyan was still listening. "Would you want your kids to grow up in a world where magic is available to everyone, where strength and power didn't require equality managers or gods or whatever?"

"Well, yeah, but my kids are grown--"

"Mine aren't..." I interrupted her, hand on my stomach as I looked at Ilyan. He stopped in place, his eyes right on me. I only saw the glistening shock in the blue orbs and felt his unrequited joy for a second before he was tackled to the ground, two of the Chosen taking him down as easily as a child.

I winced as the pain of the impact echoed through me, Wyn's Ping-Pong focus between us growing more frantic out of the corner of my eye. Ilyan didn't even fight against the burly men who had taken him down, he lay there, staring at me from the ground, tears dripping onto the grass.

'I'm going to be a daddy?'

"Yes," I said aloud, my own tears falling while Wyn cackled like a maniac beside me.

ALSO BY REBECCA ETHINGTON

For the always up to date list of super awesome books I've written, visit here:

www.rebeccaethington.com/complete-works/

THE WORLD OF IMDALIND

The Imdalind Series (complete)

Kiss of Fire, Imdalind #1

Eyes of Ember, Imdalind #2

Scorched Treachery, Imdalind #3

Soul of Flame, Imdalind #4

Burnt Devotion, Imdalind #5

Brand of Betrayal, Imdalind #6

Dawn of Ash, Imdalind #7

Crown of Cinders, Imdalind #8

Spark of Vengeance, Imdalind #9

Flare of Villainy, Imdalind #10

Imdalind Academy

The Gauntlet, Book One

Rogue Royalty, Book Two

THE WORLD OF THE OKIVAN

Of River and Raynn

CATALYST

REQUISITE

SYPHER

THE DARK WORLDS

THE THROUGH GLASS SERIES (COMPLETE)

BOOK ONE: THE DARK

BOOK TWO: THE BLUE

BOOK THREE: THE ROSE

BOOK FOUR: THE CUT

BOOK FIVE: THE LIGHT

ABOUT THE AUTHOR

Rebecca Ethington is an internationally bestselling author with over a million books sold. Her breakout debut, The Imdalind Series, has been featured on bestseller lists since its debut in 2012.

Born and raised under the lights of a stage, Rebecca has written stories by the ghost light, told them in whispers in dark corridors, and never stopped creating within the pages of a notebook.

Find me online
www.rebeccaethington.com
contact@rebeccaethington.com

THE COMPLETE IMDALIND SERIES

BOOK ONE: *Kiss of Fire*
BOOK TWO: *Eyes of Ember*
BOOK THREE: *Scorched Treachery*
BOOK FOUR: *Soul of Flame*
BOOK FIVE: *Burnt Devotion*
BOOK SIX: *Brand of Betrayal*
BOOK SEVEN: *Dawn of Ash*
BOOK EIGHT: *Crown of Cinders*
BOOK NINE: *Spark of Vengeance*
BOOK TEN: *Flare of Villainy*

THE ACADEMY BOOKS
The Gauntlet
Rogue Royalty
Broken Renegade
Reluctant Seer

Find me online in my Facebook street team! We have monthly giveaways, sneak peeks, competitions and more!